the threat

"A comic masterpiece."

—Andy Borowitz, *New York Times*-bestselling
author of *Profiles in Ignorance*

"I savored every word of Nathaniel Stein's hilarious, expertly crafted, giddily uncompromising debut novel. *The Threat* is full of pathos—loneliness, alienation, existential horror. But Stein is such a deft comedic stylist that all I experienced while reading it was joy. It's a fantastic book and I hope he writes a million more."

—Simon Rich, Thurber Prize-winning
author of *New Teeth*

"Nathaniel Stein has written a comic novel unlike anything that we have on hand recently: a small-scale exquisitist portrait of an improbable existence that has elements of both Kafka and Bruce Jay Friedman, and manages to be both appealingly absurd and strangely touching. A genuinely original book."

—Adam Gopnik, *New York Times*-bestselling
author of *Paris to the Moon*

"*The Threat* is a brilliant tour through one guy's self-obsession as he desperately tries to stay alive while also deciding why and if he really wants to—a darkly hilarious mystery about a man who finally comes to life when someone threatens to kill him. A genuinely funny novel—the kind we need more of!"

—Steve Hely, Thurber Prize-winning
author of *How I Became a Famous Novelist*

the threat

the threat

a novel

nathaniel stein

KEYLIGHT
BOOKS
AN IMPRINT
OF TURNER
PUBLISHING

Keylight Books
an imprint of Turner Publishing Company
Nashville, Tennessee
www.turnerpublishing.com

The Threat

This is a work of fiction. All the characters and events portrayed in this book are
either products of the author's imagination or are used fictitiously.

Cover and book design by William Ruoto

Library of Congress Cataloging-in-Publication Data
Names: Stein, Nathaniel, 1987- author.
Title: The threat / by Nathaniel Stein.
Description: Nashville, Tennessee : Keylight Books, [2024]
Identifiers: LCCN 2023005302 (print) | LCCN 2023005303 (ebook) |
  ISBN 9781684429691 (hardcover) | ISBN 9781684429707 (paperback) |
  ISBN 9781684429714 (epub)
Subjects: LCGFT: Black humor. | Novels.
Classification: LCC PS3619.T4754 T48 2024 (print) |
  LCC PS3619.T4754 (ebook) | DDC 813/.6—dc23/eng/20230712
LC record available at https://lccn.loc.gov/2023005302
LC ebook record available at https://lccn.loc.gov/2023005303

Printed in the United States of America

10 9 8 7 6 5 4 3 2 1

For Lesley

the threat

1

THE DEATH THREAT ARRIVED ON A MONDAY. LEVIN was settling into his evening routine, warm with the satisfaction of having changed the pants that had been dampened by a passing car on the drizzly walk home from work, and of having finished his back exercises in less than twenty minutes, and of having placed his tea in its dignified corner opposite his to-do list—which today contained the all-important item of preparing the presentation that would clinch his promotion to Mr. Adderley's former position—when from between a dental-appointment reminder and a catalogue for duffel bags tumbled the neatly addressed envelope that contained the plain little note telling him he was going to be murdered.

It was an ordinary letter-sized sheet of paper, in the center of which was a compact block of text written in a somewhat fanciful—almost girlish—cursive that contrasted strangely with its menacing words. It read:

> Mr. Melvin Levin, I'm going to kill you. You've worn out my patients for the last time and your through. My fury will rain down on you like a pack of rapid dogs and you'll be flayed. I'll smash you're head into ten million pieces and cut them and feed them to the dogs. I've got my eyes on you.

Levin was astonished. He'd never been threatened with death before. Once, in line at a coffee shop, he had been startled by a man yelling violent threats—but it had turned out the man was yelling at the person behind him. Certainly nothing in his experience could compare to the otherworldly shock that now overcame him at the sight of this brief, unelaborate note.

Could it be? Was he really going to be killed? Was it really possible that in his future there was flaying? The very idea amazed him.

He was reeling under the force of a strange and ferocious anxiety that blotted out all other sensations and didn't allow him even to have the thought, "You're panicking." It was a novel feeling that consisted mainly of his chest melting—as if it had been flooded with a corrosive poison—and also, at intervals, surges of mild pain through his legs so that they felt like they were being mangled, but gently, as though by an incompetent mangler.

He stood up and walked around the room in an attempt to inhabit this strange new anxiety and accommodate himself to it. He had to be careful with his footsteps—his downstairs neighbor complained about the sound of his walking, forcing him to tiptoe in his own home—but he was nevertheless able to do enough of this accommodational pacing to get the sensations to dissipate slightly.

But as soon as he sat down again, they came flooding back.

"So now I'll have manglings," thought Levin with annoyance. For the sensations would certainly make it impossible for him to work. And it was crucial that he finish the presentation tonight. He couldn't very well show up in Meldon's office the next day with a shrug, and say, "I'm sorry, but I had manglings." Meldon was a practical man who prided himself on working with his hands and would not understand manglings.

And yet, when the sensations did finally abate, some unaccountable impulse caused Levin to focus once again on the menacing note in order to feel the surges anew.

It was a very bad time for a death threat. A whole army of

irritations and inconveniences had recently arrayed itself in Levin's path, and even without the added problem of possibly being killed it was shaping up to be a trying week.

For one thing, his two favor-asking neighbors—between whom his tiny apartment was pincered—had both, the week before, unleashed masterpieces of favor-asking on him. First Mrs. Cohen, the elderly widow upstairs, had asked him to move one of her dense bureaus, causing him to tweak his back in what he feared was a complicated way. He was in general happy to assist Mrs. Cohen—he would even, until his busyness in recent months had made it impossible, sit with her and take in her widowly anecdotes with sympathy—but not to the extent of a back-tweaking. Next he had fallen prey to some flirting by the exerciser—the young woman whom he only ever encountered on her way back from exercising—and agreed to watch her cat while she left town. It wasn't long before he discovered that the cat, though adorable, tended to vomit. And then, just a few days ago, had come the return of the wailer—a street person who screamed loudly outside Levin's window at unpredictable times. Her absence had evidently been only a sabbatical during which she had learned additional wailing techniques, including a kind of vibrato.

And in the midst of all these small things was, of course, the huge thing: Mr. Adderley's retirement, the opening of his position, and the necessity—the absolute necessity—that Levin ascend to it.

Levin had waited nineteen years for this epochal moment. No, not nineteen: his whole life, really, all forty-nine years, had been leading to it. He felt the anticipation of those years, all that recorded hope, not as the preparation for a pleasurable release but as an intolerable burden of anxiety—as though each of those forty-nine years, with all their fevered imaginings of future joys, were stacked on top of his freshly tweaked back.

And now a death threat. Levin pulled the to-do list toward him and, with a grimace of defeat, added "death threat" to the already onerous accumulation of tasks.

How many impingements on his time could he expect from a death threat? How many impositions would be added to the slew he already faced? A trip to the police? Would he have to look constantly over his shoulder to see who was coming? Dart unpredictably into alleyways to avoid possible killers? He let out a bitter sigh. He wasn't prepared for darting, not with his back in the shape it was in.

If only the death threat could be put off until June—how much easier it would be! In June he could approach a death threat fresh-faced. In June he could give a death threat the care and attention it required. He would be happy to crane his neck around corners in June, and his back might even be in shape for darting. The threatener himself might well favor rescheduling, if it could only be explained to him—how vexing!

Levin buried his face in his hands. For it was clear, no matter how much he might wish to deny it, that the threat and all its concomitant distractions posed a serious risk to the promotion, which—though it was practically his already (and in fact many of his colleagues had already bestowed their congratulatory glances on him)—still required certain small *pro forma* tasks to be fully secured.

One was the presentation, which Meldon had requested from all candidates. A second was to come up with box questions with which to cultivate Meldon's good mood. Meldon was a woodworking enthusiast who specialized in the construction of small wooden boxes—a topic that set his normally sedate nature ablaze with passion—and it was best to approach him with some box questions prepared.

But now would Levin even have time for box questions? Let alone the presentation . . .

Still, he reassured himself, the promotion was his, even if he had to be hasty about things—even if he arrived with no box questions at all. It was true that Flemingson was making a run for it. Flemingson—a tall, gangly whistler whose whistling manner concealed a stunning propensity for wiles—had wheedled his way into contention with his sycophancy and his knickknack collection. It was part of his wiles, the collection: a constantly metastasizing cluster of porcelain animal figurines that he arranged on his desk into silly scenes that didn't make sense even on their own terms—a donkey on trial before a jury of pigeons; an elephant campaigning in front of a crowd of penguin voters. If Levin were to stoop to such tactics—an impossibility, for he looked upon them with searing contempt—he would certainly have constructed animal scenes of impeccable logic.

Nevertheless the knickknacks, which had won over the rank and file of the office who cooed over them, had been a brilliant move, Levin had to acknowledge—a masterstroke.

He supposed he should try to think of who might have sent the death threat. With a sigh, he pulled out his notebook, opened it to a fresh page, and wrote "SUSPECTS" across the top. Then, unable to resist, he underlined the word with ornate curlicues.

Who could want to kill him? The thought was inconceivable. He had lived his life with an unceasing, almost superstitious rectitude, taking great pains to avoid rubbing people the wrong way. It had been a life of unerring politeness, of profuse and precautionary apologies, of alerting a store clerk that he had been given too much change only to be excoriated by a scarf-draped woman who for some reason had felt the need to ridicule Levin's conscientiousness before the entire store—a life of reflexive accommodation, right down to the favor-askers and the noise-complaining neighbor for whom he now tiptoed in his own home like a deranged ballerina.

Other people who receive a death threat probably have reams of suspects to consider, Levin thought. Whereas he had lived his life as though with the express aim of avoiding threats—only to receive one anyway! It was characteristic of the bad luck that had met him at every turn—the bad luck of which even this competition for the promotion was an outgrowth. For in truth, by merit, he should have ascended to Adderley's position long before.

Bad luck? No. He had to admit that it was not bad luck that had held him back. It was, in fact, the rectitude that had done it—that had hemmed him in and, in the end, crippled him. Those who get ahead bend the rules, and Levin could not. How many times had he shied from an opportunity, because to seize it might have entailed the slightest risk of offending, of rankling, of disrupting, of transgressing even in the most forgivable way? How many times had he sabotaged his own small advantage out of a sense of fairness? How many times had he alerted a rival to some unseen obstacle ahead out of an overpowering fear of the guilt that might arise if he didn't?

Yes, he should already be in Adderley's position—not mired in a grunt-inducing struggle to attain it. He should have been enjoying its perks for years. The injustice had been weighing on him, and indeed was even why, if he were being honest, he had stopped his visits to Mrs. Cohen in recent weeks, instead leaving the groceries and drugstore items he picked up for her at her door—it was not his busyness that precluded his coming in, as he had told her, but that the grandmotherly praise she heaped on him during his visits had begun to disconcert him. He had begun to feel ashamed before it—as though he were deceiving her by accepting grandmotherly praise without noting that he had not yet won the key promotion on which it implicitly rested.

Not yet. Instead, for now, he had to avoid those compliments—

though there were other indignities he could not avoid. Like the superior glances of the sleek-suited lawyers who worked in the firm with offices on the building's ninth floor—the offices with the marble bathrooms which Levin had used once in an emergency—when he saw them on the elevator. They would clam up instantly at his entrance and stand in stiff dormancy, shooting occasional joke-thinking glances at one another—glances that promised that later they would make sophisticated allusions to some faux pas Levin had made.

They wronged him with those joke-thinking glances—though Levin could not really blame them for it.

And in his despair, the death threat—perched on his desk with a certain satisfaction to it, as though it were smirking at him—seemed like a gloss on his whole stunted life.

Not that his life was anything to turn your nose up at. Far from it. Even with the stunting, he was still the most prominent Melvin Levin in America. He was certain of this because he kept track of all the Melvin Levins assiduously, conducting an internet search of the name almost every night to see if the others were gaining on him. But what could he possibly fear from the pharmacist in Tulsa—on the verge of retirement anyway—or the math teacher in western Pennsylvania whose awards from the school board with their celebratory dinners merely brought a smirk to Levin's face?

The geologist was someone to keep an eye on, it was true. The geologist was, potentially, trouble. His appointment at the University of Missouri might not look like much, but he had apparently achieved many rock-related things in his thirty-seven years—accomplishments that had gained him a four-bedroom house in a nice suburb and a wife with radiant eyes whose elbows he liked to clasp in photos. And, recently, he had discovered some new rock-based phenomenon which Levin feared was rather important. It had led to many hand-shakings with important members of the geological community—and in his weaker moments, it made Levin tremble.

But only in weaker moments. After all, what were a few rock discoveries compared with his own achievements? They might not be as glamorous. Certainly no geology magazines were going to do features on them. But did that make it any less remarkable to have achieved raises in every year, even the two when very few were given out—as Levin had? Did it make it any less incredible that he was the only person in the office to receive a special greeting from the Chairman whenever he visited, except once when the Chairman was experiencing a gastrointestinal issue for which his own assistant had—without a whit of embarrassment—apologized? These were the sorts of things that weren't written about in magazines, perhaps. But they were things that would—if the geologist had any shred of awareness of the world beyond his rock collection—make him worry.

The notebook was open before him still, the page blank except for the heading, "SUSPECTS." He was wasting time. You don't receive a death threat and then twiddle your thumbs. He squeezed his eyes shut and directed all his concentration toward searching his memory for someone he might have wronged.

There was the man whose toe he'd accidentally stepped on coming out of the subway. The man—a tall, frowning hurrier with sinister, uneven baldness—had fixed Levin with a truly poisonous glare. But a death-threat glare?

He wrote: "Toe man? Unlikely."

There was Rogers, the rotund IT worker who had possibly seen Levin make an inadvertent gesture of rotundness. Levin had been demonstrating the magnitude of something by throwing his hands outward and then had seen, in the distance, Rogers's baleful glance emitting from atop his T-shirt-draped immensity. He had wondered fleetingly whether to go to Rogers and explain that his gesture had not been a reference to rotundity but had decided against it. Now all such decisions had to be doubted. The thing to do was to suss Rogers out, through indirect conversation—but was Levin up to sussing? Sussing is one of the hardest things in the world to do in ideal circumstances, and now at a moment's notice Levin was expected to take it up at the level of a master, with the highest imaginable stakes!

Annoyed, Levin wrote: "Rogers: Rotund gesture? Suss."

Then he realized, with anguish, that the mistaken gesture of rotundity was only one of a multitude of gestures that could have been misinterpreted over the years. Gesture control had never been Levin's forte.

He wrote, "Gestures," but even as he added the trailing ellipsis he knew the futility of it.

Who else? There was the neighbor who complained about Levin's walking. But Levin had responded to this man with characteristic accommodation. He had procured rugs for every conceivable pathway around the apartment, and now walked upon them with gymnastic care, even using a spare bathmat as a mobile "extender" when he needed to reach a few seldom-visited corners that had not yet been fully pathed.

There was Flemingson himself, of course. He had to be considered. His ambition—belied by his whistling manner (perhaps with cagey intent)—was huge. Of course he wouldn't mind having Levin out of the way, with the promotion on the line. And he was a dispassionate planner who engaged in long-range thinking, as evidenced by the strategic deployment of his porcelain animal figurines. Each of them seemed the result of a laborious process of consideration, during which he had squinted as his porcelain dealer held up animal after animal, shaking his head and saying, "No, it's not quite stupid enough."

But, with his whistling manner and his tall hair, he seemed incapable of threatening violence.

Levin wrote, "Flemingson? Doubtful."

And at once, Levin—looking up and down his short list—realized that he had accomplished nothing. There was not one plausible suspect, and he could sit here for hours and hours, he now knew, and not get an inch closer to one.

And suddenly he was overcome by a wave of irrepressible frustration—a frustration such as he had never felt, a frustration that coursed through his whole body, pounding at the inside of his skin. He stared at the threat, which now seemed the emblem of all the wrongs against him. Seemed the *only* wrong against him, for all the rest—the back tweak, the wailer, the favor-askers, even Flemingson's run for the promotion, even the years of squandered chances—had now receded behind the threat's enormity.

To send a death threat was a rude and thoughtless thing to do, Levin thought in anger. If you're going to kill someone, kill him! Don't make him suffer in anticipation! And certainly not when he is in the midst of a thousand other problems. Death threats are for people with the luxury of time. Or for people—like the lawyers on the ninth floor—who could, with one elegant phone call, summon a team of experts to allay all fear at once. Yes, for the lawyers, a death threat would be almost a joy! But for Levin it was one more inconvenience heaped upon the pile of them that was his existence—a thing hurled at him with the same thoughtlessness with which life had hurled everything at him. The threat was the flag planted atop the mountain of bad luck that was his life!

And in a spasm of frustration, he threw his legs forward in dual nihilistic kicks, and it seemed as though he realized before it had happened—though still too late to stop it—that the right leg would catch the wire of his lamp (had caught it), which would topple over (had toppled over), lassoing his tea and bringing it along for the smashing as though in some kind of doomsday pact.

For a moment he marveled at the complexity of the mess he had created. The shards of the mug and the lamp mixed to form a mosaic of disaster amid the expanding puddle of tea, which reached the edge of the rug in front of his desk with astonishing speed—the rug which, with slightly different placement, might have prevented the smashing. It was as though, years ago, he had played an elaborate joke on himself by rigging things just right for this to occur.

It was the threatener's first victory. Smashings were what he was counting on. *I'll smash you into a million pieces.* Oh, how he would grin with glee if he could see this, the first fruit of his hand-iwork. "He smashed his tea already," he'd say, unable to believe his luck.

Levin was unsure what to do. He wanted to wallow in the enormity of the disaster. For long minutes, he thought about wal-lowing. He looked at the mess, wondering whether to wallow or not, knowing in advance how fleeting the pleasure of wallowing would prove, and yet how marvelously fulfilling for a time, for a precious moment—when suddenly, through the open door of the bathroom, he caught his reflection in the mirror over the sink, and something in it arrested him.

He walked into the bathroom and stood before the mirror in silence.

So this was now to be the reflection of a man under the threat of death. The thought amazed him. Almost unconsciously he stood up straighter. He looked down, as though this new thought were too powerful to gaze at directly; but then slowly, almost cau-tiously, he looked back up.

Yes: it was the reflection of a man under the threat of death.

An uncanny feeling had come over the apartment. The silence

seemed to have deepened, as though a crowd had hushed all at once. Entranced, he said to himself again: *a man under the threat of death* . . .

And it was as though these words had unleashed a force that was bringing his predicament into clear view for the first time— a predicament whose enormity he was now able to marvel at, not in anxiety but in quiet awe.

What a burden had fallen upon him! Almost despite himself, he broke into a smile.

But no, that was wrong: men under the threat of death ought not to smile—at least not extraneously. They certainly can't dispense smiles left and right with the unthinking prodigality of an ordinary person. Their smiles must be elicited only by serious victories—or perhaps by sophisticated humor, the satisfaction of the most nuanced ironies.

And not only smiles, he realized with an excited flush, but all expressions would now have to be fashioned according to the death threat! He would have to affect an entire death-threatened mien and bearing . . . How much work it was all going to be!

He leaned toward the mirror and, with admirable deliberateness, began to rearrange his expression bit by bit—furrowing his brow, adding additional wrinkles to the furrowing and then taking some of them away, and making his eyes into indifferent mysterious little slits. He quickly realized the incredible difficulty of fashioning a death-threatened expression. He had, he felt, the face for it: his rather high forehead, which his tastefully receding hair had lately put on display, lent itself nicely to demonstrative wrinkling; and his regular, if perhaps somewhat bulbous, features were mobile and communicative—he was sometimes thought angry when he was not, but otherwise his expressional accuracy was fairly high. Yes: it was a face on which a death-threatened expression ought to sit quite comfortably. Still, there were many pitfalls. It was easy for it to veer toward the cartoonish or the overwrought—for a facial arrangement meant to convey profound alarm, tempered by dignified confidence, to seem instead to indicate the smelling of a nasty smell, or being on the verge of a sneeze.

Finally, after some experimentation with mouth-pursing, he found what he felt to be the proper expression. It was perfect: solemn, dignified, almost patrician—more noble resignation than fear.

Overjoyed, he turned to leave the bathroom, and, though bursting with satisfaction, he was careful to hold his expression firmly in place, not allowing a hint of his ebullience to enter it. Then, suddenly, he wheeled back around to the mirror, as if to catch himself unawares—and was pleased to see that his expression was still quite close to the way he had arranged it. Then he left the room beaming, throwing all expressional caution to the wind.

His neck ached slightly from the sudden wheeling back, and he rubbed it, annoyed at having exacerbated his troubles with this hasty action—but the annoyance quickly dissolved into an indulgent smile, accompanied by the thought: "Well, with the threat, I'll soon have to undergo greater physical risks than that, won't I?"

In the hallway, Mildred, the exerciser's cat, crossed his path. She stopped and turned to look at him—with, it seemed to Levin, a new expression on her face. "Yes," he thought, "even the cat can sense that my bearing has changed . . ."

Then she lay on her side and began one of her writhing little dances, tempting Levin to break into a dangerously unnuanced smile—but he controlled himself.

He ought to dress, too, in a way that befitted a man in such a profound situation. Here was a new challenge. In his bedroom he stared into the closet, frozen in vexation. None of his outfits seemed right for a death threat. How naïve he'd been in assembling his wardrobe, scooping up pieces willy-nilly without thinking of anything more than the price and whether they flattered whatever random notion of proper appearance happened to be flitting through his mind at that moment. Men facing a death threat can't do it that way. No wonder the lawyers hadn't given him a thought! No wonder they had looked past him with their joke-thinking glances!

So much was becoming clear all of a sudden . . . as though his life, which had seemed so unsatisfactory but whose particular flaws had been blurred and obscured, had now been thrown abruptly into focus—but at the worst time, just when the death threat would prevent him from making any real progress in rectifying it!

Then he remembered the drizzle and smiled, for his gray trench coat, inherited from a mysterious uncle, was by far the most dignified item in his wardrobe. How serendipitous! It was as though the weather were conspiring with him in the construction of his death-threat mien. The trench coat would bathe him in a delicious aura of seriousness.

Immediately he decided to go for a walk. He gave the coat an extravagant toss over his shoulder as he put it on. He would need a death-threat wardrobe for all weather, of course; the coat was only a start. But that could be safely put off until another day. Men under the threat of death can't be expected to take on everything at once!

The paths formed by the rugs he had put down to placate his downstairs neighbor were irregular, and he had to follow a wide, convoluted circle to get to the front of the apartment. At the door, he realized that he had forgotten his keys, which meant he would have to retrace the whole wide circle in order to retrieve them.

Or—he thought with mild alarm—he could simply walk straight back to the bedroom, a much shorter path over the uncarpeted hardwood floor.

He felt a perverse shiver of excitement at the plausibility of the idea. Why not? People under the threat of death can't bend over backward to accommodate every little thing...

And, with unbelievable boldness, he took a step off the rug, the contact of his sock with the bare hardwood delivering an almost otherworldly thrill. He stood there, one foot still on the rug, one venturing forward, and broke into a wide grin. It was all he could do not to burst into a cackle—but cackling wouldn't do, not when he was under threat. There would be plenty of occasion for cackling later on.

Before leaving, he looked across the room at the threat lying on the desk. He nodded slightly, with a hint of menace, as though taking leave of a despised and formidable enemy with whom a duel is scheduled and with whom in the meantime, as a matter of honor, a certain tense respectfulness must be maintained.

In the lobby of his building he wished there were a doorman to whom he could say, "I'm going out." How nice it would be to offer parting words to a doorman! If there was time—if he ended up not being killed for a while—perhaps he could look into moving to such a building.

He left in good spirits.

2

THE RAIN HAD PICKED UP SLIGHTLY. HE WALKED AIM-lessly, thinking all the time of his predicament, whose seriousness he could not quite believe. So this is what it's like to be a man under the threat of death, he thought to himself, as though it were something he had wondered about for years. What others can only guess at—he was now living.

He was struck by the newfound unfamiliarity of his surroundings. The streetscape through which he had walked so often seemed entirely different. The streets, marbled with mist and lighted from above by a sky that was strangely clouded, glowed an otherworldly silver-gray. The spectacular weather seemed as though it had been especially prepared for his adventure; those huge, unusual clouds—lit by the moon as though from within—seemed the grand emblems of the incredible drama into which he had stepped.

And Levin realized with a start: he was now a man under the threat of death walking through mysterious, rain-soaked streets. The thought filled him with tremendous excitement.

He felt that he was—quite naturally, he barely had to fashion it consciously—walking with the gait of a man under the threat of death. It was a confident and rapid walk, with a hint of urgency conveyed mainly by a slight hunching forward, and with alertness given off by occasional head-turns from side to side—but whose dominating impression was nevertheless a sense of contemplative ease, of reflection. All this he found very easily, stopping only once or twice for adjustments.

As he walked on, he kept repeating to himself the incredible but true phrase—*a man under the threat of death*—and then, turning the words around, extracted new variations—*a man who has been threatened with death, a man facing a life-and-death struggle*—and shook his head in disbelief and awe at each one. It was becoming more and more clear as he advanced deeper into his stunning new surroundings that it was not only the weather that made everything seem so different: from beneath the veil of the death threat, the world itself seemed to have been transformed—to have become strange and mysterious, filled with heretofore undreamed possibilities.

And for some reason, when he came to a particularly deep puddle that he barely avoided, he smiled and almost broke into a laugh, and thought to himself, "Careful! . . . Or do you want to get flayed?"

Just then he saw someone coming toward him. It was a small, bald man who was bounding erratically toward Levin with great energy. The threatener!

In a panic, Levin lurched toward a bench, thinking he could crouch behind it. In the uncontainable hysteria of his scurrying, he collided into a stranger's side, and barely registered that he had knocked a drink out of the man's hand. With his heart pounding, he could think only to get to the bench, and to yell as loudly as he could in the hope that someone would intervene.

But some inadvertent glance back at the bounding man, as Levin reached the bench, made him understand, in a flash, that the man—who was wearing a lanyard from which a laminated plastic card of some kind dangled on his slick jacket—was a tourist waving a brochure, in search of directions.

Levin, in a half crouch behind the bench, got up with slow, solemn care. He was mindful of the need to preserve his new dignified mien, though the unrelenting rapidity of his heartbeat made it difficult. He met the glare of the man whose drink he had spilled with only a slight flinch. "My apologies, sir," he said, pleased with the steadiness of his voice.

The drink-clutching man shook his head with contempt. Levin reached into his pocket, thinking he'd cavalierly toss him a few bills in recompense—a cavalier toss would be a fine thing!—but, losing courage, he brought his hand back out and extended it, half handshake offer and half magnanimous wave, and then, bowing slightly, said: "It was truly an accident."

But the man was already walking away, without having seen his bow—which was just as well, since that strange improvisation, Levin thought, was not exactly what it should have been. Nevertheless, he felt he'd carried off this little incident with admirable panache. He had scurried away and cowered, it was true, and in the process knocked a drink. But was it really fair to expect a man with no previous death-threat experience to be free of all cowering and drink-knocking within mere hours of receiving a threat? That kind of nonchalance would come with time.

The tourist, meanwhile, was looking on in amused puzzlement, as though he had been made privy to some strange custom normally hidden from outsiders (which in a sense, Levin supposed, he had). Levin approached him, daring to put a sway into his step, thinking that a tourist was the perfect audience for the testing of more experimental modifications to his gait, such as sways. If the experiments went awry—well, no one would hear of it but the denizens of a foreign nation.

"Can I help you find something, sir?" Levin said.

"Why were you crouching?" the man asked.

"Never mind that," Levin said with an exaggerated knowingness by which he hoped to suggest that the reason for his crouching was a joke that the tourist would not be able to appreciate.

To be asked for directions would ordinarily have caused Levin some anxiety. He felt too keenly the responsibility of it, and would take excruciating pains to be accurate. But now, having been threatened with death—now that he understood what *true* responsibility, true danger was—he took care of this little task with suave unconcern, smiling at the irony of it. Even a man under the threat of death has to pause for these sorts of mundane activities, after all!

He marveled as he watched the man bound back into the darkness, toward the wax museum. How stunned the man would be if he were to find out whom he had just asked for directions! He and his wife would sit together, blinking in shock, going over it again and again . . . "And can you imagine, I asked him for directions! *Him*, of all people!" It would be a prized anecdote for the rest of their lives.

And, sitting down on a bench, Levin realized with astonishment that *all* the people who walked past him, hurrying home from work through the escalating rain, were completely oblivious of the fact that they did so in the presence of a man facing mortal danger. To think that they were all so utterly absorbed in their petty little concerns—which, Levin thought with a thunderclap of hilarity, they took to be serious!

Though he had the urge to laugh at these people, it was to be a generous, even a compassionate laugh, not a scornful one—for in truth Levin envied them their unthreatened innocence. What wonders surround ordinary people all the time, without their having the faintest suspicion . . .

But then he realized, with appropriate chagrin, that he, too, had been oblivious until quite recently. Only a few hours ago, *he* had walked these same streets without any idea of what awaited him—without any idea of what depths of danger were even possible. Incredible! He, too, had been obsessed with his petty problems as though they actually were something. Now he saw the absurdity of it. The tweaked back, the vomiting cat, the wailer, even the promotion over which he had obsessed—it all had receded to a pleasant background buzz, and it was amazing that he could have been so vexed by these things. He had been granted a more acute sight, and from now on he would be careful to maintain that greater awareness.

He realized that he was soaking wet. The rain had intensified in the last several minutes, drenching his clothes and turning his leather shoes to sludge. He stood and began to walk aimlessly again. Even besludged, his shoes crunched the gravel underfoot satisfactorily. He didn't feel like going home, in spite of being soaked. He had a vague sense that the sight of the death threat against him might dissipate his good mood. And anyway, he should break his routine. He had to be careful about lapsing too easily into his pre-threat habits. That was what the threatener was hoping for.

He had come to a fancy restaurant that he had passed many times before but never dared to enter. Yes, how serendipitous, how right. When you're under the threat of death you have to rely on these little automatic things, your feet being smarter than you are. For it was a restaurant very much appropriate to a man under the threat of death: an imposing stone edifice, a dignified metal placard with the street number, and heavy doors that you pull with great satisfaction, their heft reminding you of the great weightiness in your life that has led to dining here. It was the kind of place where the ninth-floor lawyers would dine.

With hardly any trepidation—and thinking nothing of the diced chicken and pasta in the red tin in the fridge, which might well possibly not keep another day—he walked in.

Once inside, he noticed that his soaking trench coat was dripping onto the fine marble floor. He felt some embarrassment—but then they must be used to this sort of thing here. You never know when important business will thrust you without warning into wet situations just prior to dining.

He turned to see a coat check attended by an attractive young woman, and he knew in an instant, from the woman's expression of infinite understanding, not only that the dripping was completely excusable but that he had indeed chosen an establishment of the first rank.

She was a tall, sweet-faced woman with exquisite features, whose only evident flaw was a chin that receded slightly, as though out of modesty. But that was rendered almost comically irrelevant—as though it were ridiculous even to consider it—by her eyes, which, dark and huge, were so striking and expressive that they seemed to make a mockery of merely ordinary beauty, as though to say, "Yes, I know I'm in a beautiful face—how boring!"

In her hands was a magnificent green coat which, after holding it diagonally across her body as though somehow taking its measure—and allowing its greenness to lend a new light to her own beauty—she swept in one long and smooth gesture onto a golden hanger, all without breaking eye contact with Levin. That movement captivated him—it had all the gracefulness of art. She *danced* with the coats! It was something that could be on a stage, he thought, and the gilt border of the coat-check window indeed seemed like a proscenium: here, coats were taken and sorted, yes, but the sorting of coats in a place such as this was no trifle, but a kind of rite entrusted only to someone of great experience. Behind her, the coats of the rich and successful awaited in obedient formation.

If he had not been wearing his first-rate raincoat, he never would have dared to approach such a finely appointed coat check. Now he did so with little hesitation—though it was not, he thought slyly, merely the coat that gave him that license now.

The woman took the coat, giving no indication of any kind that she saw anything unusual or unworthy in it. And in fact, she held it aloft for the briefest moment and—Levin was certain—glanced at it with a barely perceptible expression of approval.

Levin felt it was the sign of a certain rapport between them.

She handed him a metallic chip with the number thirty-four on it. Levin fingered the exquisite chip. It was hefty, magnificently polished, and proclaimed its numeral in a dignified and regal typeface. How fine the things here were! Unable to suppress the impulse to speak his amazement aloud, he said: "Thirty-four."

Then, his cheeks turning red at his own boldness, he added, "You've chosen a number that suits me!"

Even Levin was unsure what he meant by this remark, which he had delivered with an ironic playfulness that was so uncharacteristic of him.

But the coat-check woman, her imperturbable smile widening even more, as though she had discerned some subtle cleverness in the remark, said, "Yes, indeed."

"Thirty-four!" Levin said again, smiling with even more daring irony. He had the sense that he was elaborating the private joke between them with uncontainable wit.

A finely dressed maître d' immediately showed him to his table, by no means a shabby one; in fact, he realized with a start, it was a central table, perhaps *the* central table—a table surely reserved for guests who were felt to be qualified to serve, in a sense, as representatives of the restaurant. The maître d' ratified this idea with an elegant sweep of his hand before pulling out Levin's chair with a graceful and unhurried motion.

The restaurant was the epitome of elegance. All about Levin were sumptuous cloths and leathers, glistening metallic fixtures of the utmost expense, and magnificent marble surfaces that practically begged to be stroked but that you never did—so that later you can wear a superior glance that says: "We dine among marbles and hardly look at them, let alone stroke them."

And he eyed the marble before him with a restrained smile.

He ordered a scotch on the rocks. Only when it arrived did he remember that he disliked scotch. Nevertheless, with the pleasurable resignation of noble self-sacrifice, he resolved to sip the scotch and to invest each sip with a controlled and understated seriousness. For on all sides were the men and women who dined in this restaurant as a matter of course. Not only his sips, but his whole bearing was to be judged.

From the tenor of conversational din—a deeply soothing sound— it was obvious that only elevated problems were discussed here (though perhaps the petty concerns of lower people were briefly touched upon, with subtle mocking). These were the people who would be able to understand the incredible burden that had been placed upon Levin by the death threat. For they, too, had their "death threats": business deals that would determine the flow of millions of dollars; political quandaries on whose outcomes turned the fates of peoples across the world—matters that were discussed, via leaned-in whispers and well-honed conspiratorial gestures, with the detachment and ease characteristic of those who've trafficked in them their entire lives.

Dining among these people, Levin had the sense that he had been elevated to a higher plane of existence—a plane inhabited by those concerned with only the most rarefied and refined things.

He leaned back in his chair and sighed with profound satisfaction. Though there had been a certain charm to being out among the oblivious masses, still it was a relief to be here among his fellow bearers of heavy burdens.

How much there was to study in their movements! In their bearings, in their expressions, in the way they leaned conspiratorially into one another at one moment before taking an elegant bite of their meal at the next . . . How expertly they were able to project— through all these things, but also through things more mysterious and fundamental, and far more difficult for the casual onlooker to detect—a *way of being*, something he had been in the presence of his entire life, had been immersed in without really noticing. He would like to sit here with a notebook as he observed them; better yet, with a camera—though he didn't want to look ridiculous.

And, realizing that he had inadvertently been staring at a man at the next table for some time, Levin—suppressing a shock of panic extremely quickly—merely smiled and nodded, as though to an acquaintance.

The man, an elderly fellow in a yellow bow tie, returned Levin's nod with subtlety, moving his head only slightly, his eyelids narrowing in synchrony with the nod, giving an overall impression of nuanced but nevertheless unmistakable deference.

Levin was stunned. Deference? Was it really possble that the man had given a nod of—deference? But why not? The things that govern deferential nodding—that determine all the subtle and automatic gestures of respect—are mysterious, after all. What impulse had caused Levin to move out of the way of the lawyers all these years? How was their superiority communicated? Through an aura, nothing more—an aura Levin was now exuding from his very pores.

When the server came to take his order, he took great care with his gestures and brought them off without incident.

Once or twice in the course of the dinner, he was overcome by a huge rush of anxiety, complete with the chest melting and leg manglings. It was as though there had been a sudden flash of light and he could see, in that flash, bright and unforgiving, the true and shocking change his life had undergone—and all of a sudden the notion of being flayed and smashed and murdered once again became real, terrifying him. He then had to steady himself against the marble—he would touch it just this once; perhaps he could explain himself on another occasion—and take a few extra-large sips of scotch. Everything was becoming easier as he was getting drunker.

And then he would recall, with a strange thrill, the little joke with the coat-check woman, which was like a secret between them—thirty-four, thirty-four! He would not have been able to explain the meaning of this joke, but he was increasingly unaware of that lack of understanding.

He soon had a stunning thought: Should he have brought the

threat with him? The idea sent a devilish shiver through him. He imagined the coat-check woman walking by and seeing that incredible document lying placidly on the table. He knew just how she would lean over it, transferring all the gracefulness of her coat-sorting movements to that lean—and how she would hold it aloft, like one of the coats, with the same look of instantaneous approval, though laced in this case with astonishment. And what would astonishment do to eyes such as those . . . ?

When the check arrived, though the amount was frightening, he barely even grimaced.

On the way to the coat check, fingering his fine number thirty-four, he tried to think of a clever remark to accompany handing it to her. And though he could not, he was consoled—actually thrilled—by the idea that he would have many more opportunities to hand numbers back to her with remarks that would stun and delight.

For he could now certainly eat at this restaurant as a matter of course.

He walked home with a feeling of immense satisfaction. The dinner, carried off successfully, had buoyed him. The rain had stopped, a change that he felt he had brought about by his own efforts. If any strange men were to run at him now, he would not even cower—and in fact he almost wished that one would, so he could display that spectacular non-cowering to a group of astonished witnesses.

At home he was met with the spilled tea, the broken lamp, and a fresh pile of cat vomit. He frowned, but only briefly; with the death threat and its enormity like a carapace around him, these irritations could now be felt only as a faint, almost pleasurable, tingling. They existed for him not as real problems, but as a kind of joke. He smiled, took up the mop with a glad heart, and swiped it over the mess in an ironic gesture, shaking his head as if to say, "Yes, I'm cleaning cat vomit—a man under the threat of death, no less—can you believe I have to do these things, too?"

And as he continued to mop the vomit, his expression transformed into one of serene confidence, and his mopping grew full
of verve and took on the quality almost of dance.

His thoughts again turned to the suspect list he had created.
Now all the fruitless efforts he had poured into it seemed the
height of silliness. To think that he could have been threatened by
Rogers! To think that someone like Flemingson could be involved
in a matter as serious as this! It was a joke.

No: now he knew that the person who had threatened him was
certainly not among his initial suspects, but was instead a person
from a different plane of existence: someone who existed high above
the petty squabbles characteristic of the circles in which Levin had
so far, unjustly, traveled; someone brilliant and sophisticated and—
why not admit it?—dangerous (Levin's face burned with excitement at the thought), whose ire he had unknowingly provoked.

After finishing with the vomit, he cleaned up the lamp shards
and the spilled tea, and was almost sorry when he finished.

Then he glimpsed his unfinished presentation on the desk. He
grinned at it with contempt, as if the pile of papers had tried to reproach him in a pathetically misguided way. To think that he had
come home this afternoon full of anxiety over completing it! Let
them reproach him for not having finished it. Let them withhold
the promotion, he didn't care!

It was true. It astonished him, but there it was: he did not care
about the promotion. For if he were to be denied it, then everyone
involved would only have set themselves up for the most delicious
humiliation when they learned the truth: that a man under the
threat of death, whose concerns were so far above theirs, had walked
among them, and they had repaid this man by dishonoring him.

He approached the threat, gleaming on the desk. (He had
placed it under his banker's lamp in order to cause the gleaming.)
Here was the tiny sheet that had introduced mortal danger into

his life—the nondescript object which, by its mere presence, had initiated the monumental challenge by which Levin's mettle was now to be defined.

He took it up and read it again greedily. He had thought he knew it well; but, reading it again, he realized how many nuances he'd missed. There was, for example, a small red smudge in the lower right-hand corner—which he had entirely overlooked! How brash he had been, to think he already knew the threat intimately. He had to smile at his own naïve overconfidence. He was still thinking, at times, like an unthreatened man.

And he went on staring at the threat, intent on analyzing it, without realizing that his mind was filled with a very pleasurable blankness.

Then he walked around the room for several minutes—with barely a thought to how loud his footsteps were—placing the threat on various surfaces in order to see which was best, which background could most effectively bring forth the marvelous power of its menace. The bureau, with its rich mahogany hue, was promising; the kitchen table, with the many symmetrical arrangements offered by its placemats, suggested several possibilities. But no place seemed just right, and, after realizing that this rearranging had taken the better part of an hour, he forced himself to go to bed. He needed to be sharp in the morning—not for work, but for the threat.

Was the threatener going to bed now too? Levin felt a strange warmth as he imagined the threatener in his lair—no doubt a dark and wood-paneled lair, hidden behind some false door, filled with his expensive spying equipment, and perhaps containing a large poster of Levin himself, to remind the threatener of why he worked so hard.

The wailer started up almost as soon as he laid his head on the pillow, but her wails hardly bothered him. He fell asleep quickly, drifting off to the image of dozens of knives falling onto him, each with a delicious sting.

3

IN THE MORNING, LEVIN WAS ONCE AGAIN ANXIOUS. Under the harsh light of day, the fact that someone wanted to kill him seemed again very unpleasant. The manglings in his legs were back, and so was the chest melting, and he had to wait several minutes in bed for them to dissipate. It seemed his whole being had been retaken by nervousness.

He left his bedroom, walking with great care on the rugs.

In the living room he was greeted by one of the lamp shards which he had evidently neglected when cleaning the night before—a remnant of the mess which, then, he had looked upon with such superior indifference. Now the sight of the shard startled him. He couldn't stop himself from imagining a shard like that one piercing his skin, a thought that made him jump in fear—such a contrast to the pleasant stings of the knives the night before!

What had happened to him overnight? It was as though the reservoir of strength he had located within himself had evaporated.

The sight of the unfinished presentation on the desk gave him another start. Had he really decided to forgo completing it? The decision, which he had undertaken with such unconcern the night before, now seemed insane. No presentation! The disordered pile of papers, which he'd taken an almost perverse pleasure in ignoring as he went to bed, now seemed the emblem of the crazed, drunken being who, in the guise of Levin's body, had done all these wild, outrageous things.

In the bathroom, as he brushed his teeth, he paused from time to time and tried to see once again in his reflection the death-threat mien that had come so naturally to him the night before. Where was it? When he finally caught a glimmer of it—more feeling than image—he set the toothbrush aside entirely and leaned toward the mirror with almost frantic purpose. He furrowed his brow in great seriousness. Yes, there was another hint of it!

He must not forget that he was now a man under the threat of death. Recalling the way the phrase had been so helpful the day before, he again intoned it aloud: "A man under the threat of death," and felt a surge of excitement enter his body through some portal opened by the words. Yes, this was the way to do it . . .

He said it again, feeling another small surge of excitement, and this time he tried to take hold of the excitement when it showed itself, to seize it and drag it into the full view of his consciousness. He repeated it again and again—"A man under the threat of death . . . a man under the threat of death," each time gaining new strength, until finally he felt it in full bloom: the dignified mien of the man who bears on his back the most solemn of problems as if they are nothing.

He finished brushing his teeth with gusto.

In the lobby of his office building, two of the lawyers stepped into the elevator with him, and Levin flushed with anxiety, recognizing his first great test.

He moved to the side of the elevator with swift, precise steps, so that the three of them were standing in a triangle of satisfying geometric precision, of which Levin had been the chief architect. Levin was—by pure accident, though he was not unable to enjoy the fact—standing side by side with one of the lawyers in back, rather than on his own in the triangle's lonely front vertex.

He stood perfectly still, focusing all his considerable concentration on maintaining a dignified bearing. It was difficult, draining work. Dignified standing would come more naturally with time, he reasoned. It would be second nature before long, and anyway most truly dignified men probably still check that they're doing it right now and again, if only out of wistful nostalgia for the time when their dignified bearing first came to them.

Though he had a powerful urge to check the lawyers' glances—to see whether they were free of the usual condescending mirth—he suppressed it, fearing that any glance-checking would throw off his dignity maintenance. He contented himself with imagining that it must be so, that their glances were joke-free. Why, after all, should the lawyers be any different than those strangers who, the night before, had nodded at him with such awestruck deference?

After a moment, he relaxed enough for their conversation to drift into his awareness.

"Which is obviously going to be a pain in the ass," the lawyer with the sharp chin was saying.

"That's true," replied his deep-voiced colleague. "Nothing could be worse than that."

It seemed to Levin that they were speaking a bit more freely than usual.

"*I* certainly can't think of anything more unpleasant."

"But I can think of a few things more *pleasant*. Hemorrhoids, for instance."

"Or alimony hearings."

"That's right," the other said, smiling knowingly.

"Or threats . . ." Levin said.

There was a sudden silence. Levin had stunned himself by speaking. For a moment, the elevator itself seemed to have stopped—but it was only the tremendous force of shock he had unleashed with those unexpected words.

But that's what men with serious problems do, Levin reasoned—they shock themselves, again and again, and bear each shock with perfect equanimity.

The lawyers looked at him with ambiguous expressions, which they fixed on Levin for several seconds as if for the purpose of giving him a chance to discern their obscure meaning. They were nonplussed, to be sure, by the interjection—but was there not also a hint of admiration in their looks? Was there not a sense that they, too, were evaluating something—whether a new member had joined their ranks . . . ?

The deep-voiced lawyer gave a slight smile. "Yes, certainly."

When the elevator opened on the fourth floor, Levin stepped out beaming.

In the hallway, he paused to calm himself. The thought that he was coming to work without having finished his presentation now came to him as a maniacal thrill—a kind of transgressively gratifying nudity. How stunned they would all be—and how ready he was now to revel in that stunnedness! Their mouths would gape, struggling to articulate their disbelief: "No presentation?!" Whereupon he would unleash a coy shrug that would stun them anew.

He planned to treat his colleagues with generosity and benevolence. He wanted to reassure them that, though he had undergone a great change, he had no objection to mingling with them and even—from time to time—socializing. To convey this, he tried to adjust his dignified bearing slightly in order to incorporate this subtle but important note of egalitarianism.

But when he was through the door, and the fluorescent array of cubicles was before him, he felt a rush of nervousness. Should he have called ahead to warn them that he would be coming to work today with a new bearing?

Rogers, the rotund IT man, walked out of a supply room with his dragging gait—he always walked as though he had weights attached to his ankles—and Levin couldn't help breaking into a wide smile at the thought that he could have supposed this blundering doofus to have been the threatener. The idea that the threatener could walk so draggingly, and wear draping, garish T-shirts—well, it was the thought of a man with so little death-threat experience that Levin could not help but be amused by his own naiveté.

His colleagues were clustered in a gaggle around Flemingson's cubicle—a familiar sight. No doubt Flemingson had debuted a new animal scene. Levin should have expected that. Silently, he upbraided himself. Certainly, given his current challenges, he would have to start anticipating more unexpected things than Flemingson doing new animal scenes frequently as the promotion decision neared!

Flemingson, with his tall hair and whistling manner—for even when not whistling, he spoke with pursed, whistle-ready lips—was centered among a group of rapt colleagues who had been arranged around him in a kind of tableau of admiration, the whole scene illuminated by an overhead fluorescent light that seemed to have been specially brightened, as though Flemingson had gotten in touch with the maintenance people that morning and said, "I'm going to do a tableau later."

In normal times, a new animal figurine might have caused Levin some distress. Now, by contrast, he quickly steadied himself. Let them ogle the new figurine; let them enjoy themselves with it. Their lives were barren of marvels, so let them take them where they could.

He approached the group with serene confidence.

"So, what's the new one, a giraffe with glasses?" he said, delighted with the sarcasm of his tone—a delight that was only barely undermined by the realization that Flemingson had in fact brought in a giraffe with glasses a couple weeks before, and that this image was not the finely calibrated parody that Levin had supposed himself to have struck upon.

"He was mugged last night," said a beautiful green-eyed woman who worked in customer service and who had positioned herself at Flemingson's side. "While he was walking home from his book club . . . two men came out of nowhere . . ." She looked to Flemingson as though expecting to receive some kind of accolade for the accuracy of her recitation.

Flemingson was, however, compelled to make a correction. "It was a play-reading club."

Now that Levin understood what was going on, the tableau took on a troubling new cast. The expressions that he had taken for figurine admiration were instead revealed to be ones of deep sympathy. Some of the colleagues were cradling their heads in their hands as though they had become heavy with the pain of Flemingson's experience. The green-eyed customer-service rep— Sophie was her name, Levin remembered—whose eyes always had a certain tear-like glassiness to them, had widened those eyes and, by placing the rest of her features into a mode of sympathy, had rendered them even more beautiful by the sudden congruity they had with their surroundings.

Levin stood back, knowing that he had to calibrate his expression quickly. There was something unseemly about this display. To think that a mugging constituted real danger! But it was also true that these people could not be expected to know better; they could not be expected to know what makes great men tremble, and that it doesn't involve petty robbery.

He stood as tall as he could, and did his best to forge two expressions at the same time: a smile of indulgent permissiveness, as of an uncle who is pretending to be oblivious while he allows the children to engage in some unwholesome game; and an expression of sympathy for Flemingson's ordeal that was sullied by just the right amount of irony, as though to say, in a slightly sarcastic tone, "Really? A mugging? How very scary!"

Then, in a sudden inspiration, he underscored his aloofness by crossing his arms in front of his chest. He felt enormously pleased as he waited for his marvelous indifference to be noticed by the others.

"Tell him how it happened!" said Leonard—a mustachioed, plaid-wearing accountant with florid cheeks who was leaning forward on elbow-planted arms in great eagerness. It was not remarkable that Leonard should be enthused by something like this. He was known for his enthusiasms, obsessions he would develop and follow passionately for weeks at a time—for a certain movie or for locating a printer that had gone missing from the office— and when he was in the midst of these enthusiasms, his cheeks would flush and his tongue would stick out like a schoolboy in the process of acing a test. That Leonard should be enthused by the mugging was therefore totally meaningless.

But the others had no excuse.

Flemingson told his story again with energetic gestural accompaniment, jabbing his hand to illustrate the muggers' knives. He was deploying his gestures with more satisfaction than they warranted. It was quickly clear that he had only two—the knife jab, and a holding up of both hands that was meant to illustrate his own unshakenness—and was simply moving them to different areas around him.

"Yes, that must have been quite something," Levin said, smirking.

"What was the knife like?" asked a head-cradling woman.

Flemingson paused. "Long," he said finally.

So there had only been one knife between the two of them, Levin thought.

"And how long did it last?" someone asked.

"Probably ten or twelve seconds—but it felt like minutes."

There was another smattering of awed approval at this banal observation. You learn about seconds lasting for minutes pretty early on when you receive a death threat, Levin mused—and yet, for these rubes, it was the sort of observation that would pass for wisdom. How pleasant for them, in their Edenic wonderland!

He tried to put some of this wistfulness into his expression, but it was becoming more difficult. The display was becoming more unseemly. The expressions of sympathy were becoming more involved. To the head cradling and wide-eyed stares were now being added—in small numbers, to be sure, but they were unmistakable—gasps and shudders.

He could have these gasps and shudders if he wanted them, of course. The death threat would garner those and far more. He could have outright weeping, tears that would flow as reliably as if they came from a faucet. And he could have, especially, the glassy eyes of the green-eyed woman turned upon him—those eyes that were made for sympathy, masterpieces of sympathy, which were now being wasted on this picayune mugging while a death threat stood by untapped. It was as though the greatest soprano in Vienna had never been allowed to sing Mozart.

Levin could, if he so wished, bask in the glow of sighs and gasps and weeping for hours.

But he would never reveal the threat to them, of course. Such an inappropriate display of power would be the height of vulgarity. You don't detonate an atomic bomb over a primitive village whose inhabitants are plotting a slingshot-powered coup against you.

Instead, he decided to speak with great subtlety. "Yes, there are all kinds of dangers," he said, and inclined his head upward, gazing at the ceiling.

"Of course, at the time, you're acting on instinct," Flemingson was saying. "You don't truly appreciate the level of danger you're in. Only afterward, when you're looking back . . . and it hardly seems to have been real . . ."

The green-eyed woman placed her slender fingers on Flemingson's elbow and began to rub it gently.

"I've been threatened," Levin said suddenly.

They all turned to look at him. There was a heavy silence. Levin noticed with some annoyance that the green-eyed woman, though she had turned to face Levin like the others, was still rubbing Flemingson's elbow, as though the elbow-rubbing had a certain momentum to it irrespective of turnings.

"A death threat," Levin went on. "I received it in the mail yesterday."

Levin again permitted a stunned silence to prevail for several seconds, an expression of placid confidence on his face.

However, he could sense that he still didn't have their full attention. A few were trying on smiles, as if to test whether he were joking, while others were looking around to try to get some idea of how to react.

"They say they're going to flay me . . ." Levin closed his eyes, for a moment losing himself in the intoxication of the idea of being flayed, but then quickly recovered himself, and added, "and that they've been watching me for some time. It's only a matter of time before I meet my violent death."

Flemingson smiled. "I see . . . some dry humor . . ."

The others relaxed immediately. They were obviously ready to believe Flemingson an expert on subtle humor.

"It's not a joke!" Levin almost yelled. "Don't you understand? Don't you understand that I'm going to meet my violent death?"

They were staring at Levin, astonished and disconcerted. So let them be astonished and disconcerted, Levin thought with a devilish inward smirk. Let them get a taste of real life!

"But I'm not giving it a thought," Levin went on, shrugging with balletic grace. "These are just the sorts of things you have to deal with when you're in the public eye!" Levin flushed at these words, but then decided that if asked what he meant by "public eye," he could mention the two industry conferences he had spoken at, where in fact there had been enormous crowds which easily could have seen Levin's speech on the monitors in the lobby area.

"It sounds like you have the right attitude," Flemingson said.

"So there's a note?" Leonard, the enthusiast, asked.

"Yes. I don't have it with me. But I have to get something from my apartment anyway," Levin said, packing his things with great haste. "I'll bring back the death threat if I remember."

And he left the office and ran to his apartment as fast as he could.

When he returned twenty-five minutes later, after taking a moment to catch his breath in the lobby—and thinking that his profuse sweating would pass, through his confident bearing, as something unrelated to the threat or his rush to retrieve it, perhaps a gland issue—he walked into the office with an air of incredible calm and self-assurance.

The group had dispersed. He wanted to gather them back, but without taking any extravagant action. So he began wandering among the cubicles in a purposefully aimless fashion, as if he were looking for something he had misplaced, and, when he reached certain cubicles, he muttered in an offhand way—as if he had only just remembered it in the course of looking for his misplaced item—"Here's the threat . . ."

After completing this wandering walk, he came back to the center table and waited for the group to regather. But the only person who came over was Marla, a floral-dress-wearing, middle-aged administrative assistant whose large head had something floral about it too, popped up from her dress, bobbing in anticipation. Her huge gray glasses intensified her constant look of expectancy, as though adding a second set of wide eyes.

"Let's see it!" she said.

Levin frowned. It ought to be the same group that had listened to Flemingson's story. And if he had to pick candidates to be the lone witness of the threat's debut, then Marla, with her blunt and uncalibrated excitement, would certainly be last on the list.

Looking around with some anxiety, Levin cleared his throat

and called out: "I've got it here!" Then, after a moment, he was forced to add, "The threat!" Then he looked off to the side as if it didn't concern him very much whether people came over or not.

Frustratingly, only one other person came—Leonard, the enthusiast. He was rubbing his hands in readiness for an enthusiasm. But the threat didn't belong among his enthusiasms. To class it with them would be like decorating a kitschy living room with one of the sacred treasures of an ancient church.

Levin again looked around, alarmed now, wondering whether he could possibly call out again, when, to his relief, another person drifted over: Dennis, a sour, crew-cut, monosyllabic accountant with a long nose framed by deeply etched vertical lines on either side of it that gave his face a look of permanent skepticism, and with a dour personality that he had seemingly developed in order for his face to make sense.

It was not quite Flemingson's tableau. Not only was the composition off, this group only a pathetic echo of the one that had lavished such decadent sympathy upon Flemingson's petty trauma; but their manner, too, Levin now realized, was all wrong. Marla was chewing gum. Before a death threat! And the others, gumless, were no better—they were slumped in their chairs in the most casual manner, their mouths agape, their eyes flashing with ravenous greed as though he were about to set before them not something so solemn and dignified as a death threat but rather one of the gaudily decorated cakes with which they celebrated one another's birthdays. This was Marla's specialty, bringing in those flowery cakes, and he eyed her with resentment for bringing to an occasion that should have been sanctified by awed hushes her cake aura.

It would be better at least to announce some ground rules—to ask them to spit out their gum and sit upright with the attentive respect that a death threat deserved. But even that was impossible. He was on the point of taking up the threat with a resigned air—he could sigh as though feeling regret on their behalf, shake his head with pity, and say, "I'm sorry, I've made a mistake"—but then he felt a new resolve harden within him. When facing a death threat, you have to make do with the resources at hand. He would surely soon face greater challenges than inadequate threat audiences. Forcing away his hesitations, Levin placed the threat on the table before them with terrific dramatic flair.

As soon as the incredible sheet touched down, he drew back his hands and clasped them into an anticipatory mass.

Their ogling was far from a disappointment. True, it did not reflect the extreme shock that was called for—you couldn't expect them to understand at a glance, as Levin had, what was before them—and their faces were more expressive of puzzlement than anything else. But the sight of so many eyes fixed on the threat—the startling newness of the image—nevertheless gave Levin a charge of thrilling energy.

Marla's nostrils began to flare, and she leaned back slightly. Levin, thinking these motions might presage a sneeze, jerked his hands forward into a position to be ready to grab the threat. His heart was pounding.

But it was soon clear that no sneeze was coming.

"We should be careful about sneeze motions," Levin said, with some shortness.

Suddenly Leonard grabbed the threat.

Levin was shocked. He could barely breathe. He jumped from his chair and stood behind Leonard, his mind racing to determine what to do in response to this emergency. Should he grab it out of Leonard's hands, risking damage? Or rather try to get him to relinquish it with calm coaxing? What do you do when your baby is in the hands of a madman? What an idiot he had been! To have been lured into laying the threat before a gaggle of uncultivated baboons! It was a lapse in judgment that could not be allowed to happen again.

But before he could decide what to do, he noticed something even more distressing: Leonard was reading the threat aloud in a squinting, mumbling monotone that barely moved his lips and resembled the way you might read a note the landlord taped to your door about hallway recarpeting.

It was a scandal. For the threat to be read in such a manner was such a stunning profanation that all the other outrages, all the gum-chewing and rough pawing and false sneeze motions, suddenly seemed bits of high refinement by comparison.

Now he must act. With a delicate but nevertheless decisive motion, Levin took the threat from Leonard's hands and read it aloud in the clear, stentorian tone that the occasion demanded.

When he finished, he looked around at his listeners, ready to take in their intoxicating sympathy.

"Huh!" Marla said.

"Remarkable," Leonard added.

Levin was puzzled. Was it merely a matter of giving the slow-witted more time to take in such a monumental thing?

"Who sent it?" Leonard asked.

These words were an injection of something venomous into Levin's abdomen. "I don't know," he said sharply.

"You know, I wouldn't worry about it," Marla said.

Levin turned to her, his face clouded with a fury that was close to despair. "What are you talking about?"

"My brother-in-law got into a tiff with a contractor who started calling up the house and threatening him. Long story short, nothing came of it."

Levin buried his head in his hands, allowing himself a lengthy refuge in the oblivion that resulted.

Then, gathering his strength, he looked up from the salving darkness of his enclosed hands and cast his gaze around the room in search of Sophie, the green-eyed woman who had given

Flemingson such sympathy during his mugging tableau. He had the sense that she would know how to react to the threat—that among these barbarians she alone, with her glassy eyes that had been as though constructed to exude sympathy, would imbue the proceedings with the proper decorum. Perhaps he could make a joke to justify inviting her, saying something like, "Maybe we could add a set of green eyes . . ."

But she was nowhere to be seen.

Well, they were rubes, Levin told himself consolingly—and why would he expect rubes to appreciate the profoundness of a death threat? If he wanted to know which pizza restaurant to go to, these were the people to approach. But if he wished for the suffocating burden of a life-and-death matter to be perceived and understood, he would have to stay within his own echelon.

Levin put on an ironic air and said, "Yes, yes, it's nothing, nothing at all," and started to pack up the threat, considering as he did so whether to say something clever and slightly wounding—something that would puzzle them now, perhaps, but impress itself on their memories so that, years later, they would look back on it with long-delayed smarting. They would see, all at once, with the force of a deathbed revelation, how Levin had represented a glimpse of hidden dimensions of life—dimensions to which they themselves had never had access—and how they had spurned him out of their own unforgivable ignorance.

"It looks like there are some spelling issues," Dennis said.

Levin, in the process of carefully folding the threat, froze as though he had been struck. "Here," Dennis said, and, not waiting for Levin to put the threat back down, he touched it with his index finger and pushed it gently all the way to the table—an outrageous violation that inspired in Levin a feeling not so much of fear as of a kind of nausea, as though an elderly stranger's hand had been discovered creeping up his thigh.

"He misspelled 'patience,'" Dennis said.

Levin merely stared, with a look of mild scolding, as though at an unbelievably brazen breach of etiquette, one so flagrant and vulgar that all you can do is stare scoldingly—to say something is so unnecessary that it would itself be a small vulgarity—and let the shame unleashed by the stare permeate the room.

"It should be 'e-n-c-e,'" Dennis added, pathetically misreading Levin's stare.

Levin adjusted his expression at once. Scolding stares were wrong—what he needed to do was to put on his superior smile. He must remember that all these quibblings were to him nothing more than an amusement.

"And he's mixed up 'your' and 'you're,'" Leonard said. "See, here and here," he added, pointing needlessly back and forth between the two instances.

"Point those out to me again," Levin said with terrific cuttingness.

But Leonard was too caught in the grip of a nascent enthusiasm to notice. "And here," he said, his cheeks beginning to flush to their enthusiasm shade, "where it says, 'like a pack of rapid dogs.' See that? See that? He must mean *rabid* dogs!"

There was no doubt about it—the threatener could not have meant to specify that the dogs were rapid.

Levin widened his superior smile.

"And this is a bit awkward, too," Dennis said, pointing. "'My fury will rain down on you like a pack of rapid dogs.' For one thing, is it like rain or is it like a pack of dogs?"

"That's called a mixed metaphor!" said Marla.

Levin's smile suddenly felt cumbersome on his face. He was having trouble maintaining it with the same naturalness as before. He tried to increase its intensity, but seemed only to contort his face further in the wrong direction.

"'I've got my eyes on you' seems out of place, at the end here," Dennis said, "like he forgot to put it in and tacked it on at the end."

"It's poor composition!" Marla added.

"It lacks a closing sentence," said Dennis.

Levin, who had the sense that he had stood in stoic repose while a cliffside disintegrated over his head, felt the need to address them.

"Look, for threats, it's . . . There are different rules . . . you can't apply rules in the same way when threats are . . ."

Levin stopped, because he could tell that Dennis was ready to point out another flaw. Levin was able to put him off with a glare. At least his glares were working.

Leonard, peering at the threat, narrowed his eyes. "And what about this red smudge?"

"The red smudge is nothing!" Levin exploded.

The others, stunned by his sudden vehemence, all receded slightly, as though they were connected to a complex marionette structure whose strings had been slackened.

"I know all about the red smudge," Levin added in a calmer tone, pleased at having regained control of the situation.

Levin turned away from them and made a few gestures of resuming a task. The others scattered back to their desks.

Alone, he nevertheless felt himself simmering. He looked down at the death threat and grimaced. He now saw nothing but its flaws. The rubes, like a broken clock, could be right on occasion. It was not only a matter of spelling and grammar, but the cheap paper stock, the childish handwriting—it all bespoke an unforgivable shoddiness.

He was furious. He deserved a death threat of far higher quality. He deserved a death threat not only of impeccable style, letter-perfect and expressed with elegant concision, but of terrifying images constructed with painstaking care—an example to other threateners. Something of which respectable people, though fiery with indignation that Levin should have such a thing foisted on him, would have to admit, "Well, the fellow can put together a threat, there's no question about that."

He deserved a threat of some professionalism—a threat that sparkled with menace! Not this shoddy production—something that barely deserved the name "threat."

He thought of the fine metallic number he had been given at the fancy restaurant to check his coat—the numerals forming the "thirty-four" which had been so crisp and stately, their grooves fit for long sessions of rubbing. (For those who had the time for such things!) And could he show this threat, with its unconcealable shabbiness—which even the rubes had seen at a moment's glance—to the coat-check woman, who handled those fine numbers all day? He would have to offer a thousand explanations, murmured through cheeks burning with embarrassment, "It's not like your numbers, of course . . ."

Perhaps—Levin thought, trying to calm himself—it was the threatener's first threat. Only that could really justify such flagrant shoddiness. But then that only meant that he ought to have taken greater care with it. And anyway, Levin deserved a sophisticated threatener with a great deal of threatening experience behind him.

Surely were one of the lawyers to receive a death threat, it would not be from a rookie dipping his toes into threatening for the first time. It would be sleek and unimpeachable—written on fine, expensive paper that could be slapped down in front of anyone and elicit nothing but ogling, awed and terror-filled ogling of the most satisfying kind! And even if by chance it contained some flaw—by a shocking oversight for which the threatener would be reprimanded, though his own humiliation would be reprimand enough—then no one would dare to point it out. Everyone would ignore it out of an unspoken sense of decorum.

Then again, perhaps the real difference between him and the lawyers was the care *they* took in choosing the company with which they mixed. What a mistake he had made in bringing the threat before that crew! And he had thought it would suffice to lay down a few imprecations about taking it in with respect! From now on, he simply had to be more careful about the environments into which he introduced the threat.

Somewhat calmed by this resolution, Levin looked up, and his gaze met the door of Meldon's office. He realized that he owed it to Meldon to alert him to the impingements and scheduling issues that might result from the threat. In fact, he had actually been remiss in not marching straight to his office first thing in the morning and briefing him on the matter.

And Levin suddenly felt a great affection for Meldon welling up within him. For with the threat, he had gained a certain newfound collegiality with his boss. He had joined Meldon on the higher plane of existence—the plane for men whose concerns encompass life and death. (In a sense, Levin was on an even higher plane, since Meldon, though his responsibilities were substantial, really dealt only with money—in vast sums, perhaps, but could even the greatest sum of money count for more than a human life? Nevertheless, Levin would not press such an advantage, even in his thoughts.) With Meldon he could consider the threat on the level that it deserved—and let the rubes concern themselves with the snack cabinets and what games to play on their computers.

As he walked to Meldon's office, Levin made a broad gesture of apology toward all his coworkers, a wide sweeping of his hands accompanied by a sheepish grin. Passing Marla at her cubicle, he ran his hand over the surface of her desk, a kind of avuncular caressing to indicate that he still held them all, if not exactly in esteem, then in sincere and almost paternal affection.

4

MELDON'S DOOR WAS AJAR, AND LEVIN COULD SEE that he was absorbed in some documents. Nevertheless, without hesitation, he knocked on the open door with a series of strong, clear, unapologetic taps. Meldon looked up with uncharacteristic attention and gestured Levin inside with an expression of slight annoyance but one not devoid of respect either, of the kind a troll might give to someone who has figured out his riddle.

Meldon's office was decorated on all sides by many of his most prized boxes. Shelves and tables were covered with boxes, and it was unclear whether they were from his own workshop or were famous boxes from history, or a mix. Levin had not prepared box questions, but, to acknowledge his newfound collegiality with Meldon, he gave the boxes a few appreciative glances, and even fixed his attention on one particular box for several seconds as if in fascination, before sitting in the chair facing Meldon's desk. Levin had no trouble finding a posture of extraordinary ease, as befitted his new status.

Though unsure whether small talk was appropriate among higher-plane people before getting down to life-and-death business—on the one hand, to waste their incredibly precious time in the face of something profound seemed wrong; on the other hand, the bit of wasted time, the gesture toward the quotidian, might be precisely what was called for to fix the attitude of nonchalance that those on the higher plane brought to such things as death threats—he took the risk, without much anxiety, of launching directly into his predicament. "I've been threatened," he said.

He said it with the cool unconcern of one who receives many death threats, a feint not without some daring, for Meldon—though perhaps not himself the recipient of many threats—no doubt knew people who got them in piles.

Then Levin took the threat from his jacket and placed it on Meldon's desk—a maneuver that necessitated a rather undignified leaning, his sleeves sweeping the desk in a vulgar way, but he was able to reattain his position of fabulous ease with amazing speed. He leaned back and said, "The spelling problems are no doubt on purpose—to suggest how erratic he is."

Meldon took the threat in his hands—barely causing Levin any panic, for you have to extend trust to the people who deserve it, out of respect but also out of concern for your own mental well-being; you simply can't live without letting go of the all-encompassing concern from time to time—and narrowed his eyes as he read it.

"I see," Meldon said, looking up. "That's something."

Levin looked at Meldon expectantly, awaiting his next pronouncement.

After the silence persisted, Levin added: "It's a death threat."

Meldon took the threat in his hands again—obviously he had read it with too much haste the first time—and narrowed his eyes even more. Levin took some quiet satisfaction in having elicited this rather extreme eye-narrowing.

Meldon put down the threat. "It's quite disturbing. And what about your presentation?"

Levin was puzzled. His mind raced as he tried to discern what Meldon was communicating to him. Was he speaking in some kind of code? Was he trying to indicate that Levin had breached some aspect of etiquette? That you don't bring life-and-death concerns up in this fashion? That there was a special time and place for them—or a special way of introducing them?

Or—and Levin smiled broadly as he realized that this was the far more likely, in fact the undeniable, case—wasn't this just what Levin had been expecting? That those for whom life-and-death concerns are no more unusual than getting the morning's paper would treat those concerns with something less than the gravity that ordinary people would . . .

Levin sat up taller in his chair and puffed up his chest slightly. He understood that he was now to collaborate with Meldon on the joke he was making of the situation—to play his part in the little show they were putting on for no audience, a divine burlesque in which the profound concerns that marked their lives were treated as if they did not even exist.

"Yes, yes, the presentation," Levin said, with an inner chuckle. He wanted to display his inner chuckle to the greatest extent possible, and he gave his puffed-up chest the slightest shimmying motion.

"Do you have it?" Meldon asked with perfect seriousness.

"Well, no—because . . ." Levin eyed the threat, thinking that to invoke it outright could spoil the game, but that to eye it must be permissible, especially if the eyeing was accompanied by an ironic expression that said, "Forgive me this little vulgarity."

"I see," Meldon said, all graveness. "Well, I suppose if you have it tomorrow."

"Yes, yes, the presentation, tomorrow," Levin said, almost daring to wink, but stopping himself when his gaze crossed the boxes behind Meldon. To wink in the presence of the boxes seemed a step too far, at least for now.

Meldon turned his attention to another pile of papers, signaling that the meeting was over. Levin was a bit disappointed, since he had been enjoying their charade so much. He wondered if he could insert one last little sally, one more extravagant non-reference to the threat accompanied by the perfect ironic glance, as a kind of finale. But, seeing how quickly Meldon had reabsorbed himself in his papers—a master of seriousness!—he held himself back (for Levin was not so uncouth as to ignore a signal) and instead lingered before one particularly distinguished box (a small and graceful mahogany one with golden inlay) and put on an expression of deep concentration, as though to mark the transition from their burlesquing back to the sobriety necessary for reentry among the uninitiated.

Just as he was about to walk out, Meldon added: "And call the police about your threat there."

Levin froze. He wondered if he had heard correctly. Had Meldon suggested he go to the police about the threat? But if so, that undermined everything—destroyed their whole charade.

Certain that it was a joke of some kind, even if he did not yet understand it, Levin raised his eyebrows and grinned with irony. "The police," he said.

"Yes," Meldon said, with, if indeed it was a joke, an unbelievable degree of dryness. "That way, you get it off your mind."

But, Levin thought as he walked back to his desk in a daze, no one was capable of such dryness.

Levin was stunned. The police? Could Meldon seriously think that the police would take care of it—would, as he had so inexplicably vulgarly put it, "get it off his mind"? If Meldon wished to stop treating the threat with the winking indifference that their game stipulated, then Levin was quite ready to grant a reprieve—devilish games can be played only so long before they tempt one to insanity—but in that case the threat ought to be treated with the sanctity it deserved. Not with a half-thinking, dismissive remark about—the police! It was a desecration.

He imagined going to the police station and sitting in a waiting room among the masses, many of them unthreatened. It was no place for him. Perhaps if there was some kind of special area for those with higher burdens—for victims of high crimes, of embezzlement and espionage, of years-long subtle schemes. Perhaps there *was* such a place, and Meldon assumed he was already aware of this.

Nevertheless, whatever the explanation, Meldon's dizzying violation of their game left him feeling deeply dismayed.

The rest of the day was poisoned by an untraceable frustration. His back pain flared up, and he had to wait almost half an hour for the lactation room—where Meldon allowed him to do his back exercises in privacy—to become available to him. It was a crime—he should have his own office!

He tried to cheer himself by thinking of the consolations that awaited him. As soon as he got home, he would study the threat closely, analyze it further—a suitable intellectual occupation—and then dine in the fancy restaurant, where in all likelihood they would display him again at the center table, from which he would put on a show of magnificently dignified eating and drinking that would have the fashionable set agog.

But something about these consolations now struck him as hollow.

He caught a glimpse of Rogers, the rotund IT man, slinking out of a supply closet and crossing the office. Rogers stopped, turned to Levin, and the two locked eyes for a moment. Rogers glared. Levin blanched in fear.

There could be no denying it, Levin now had to admit: Rogers might well be the threatener. How shameful! How ignominious! To be threatened by a person such as Rogers, with his draping T-shirts, with his thin facial hair that traced unconventional patterns around his face, and with his dragging, slinking walk . . . Were those garish T-shirts truly to be the harbinger of his death? Was he to die under their banner—Rogers's uncouth rotundity forming Levin's last image of the world?

Levin made fists and ground his nails into his palms as hard as he could. But when he opened his fists he saw, with some disappointment, that there was no blood.

So let him come. Was death any less profound for having been inflicted by a Rogers? Would his stabs be rendered any less painful by his garish T-shirts—his flaying any less terrifying by his rotund slinking? No. He was as dangerous as any sleek operator.

Let him come, Levin thought with perverse relish. Even if it be Rogers. Even if it be someone draped in even more embarrassing shirts. Let him come; let him stab Levin in the eyes in front of all his coworkers, who would look on in dumb shock, pathetically unable to administer any kind of medical assistance even if terror hadn't stunned their awkward limbs into total paralysis! Let them watch as Levin sank to the floor!

Let them weep as Levin—stoic to his last breath—gazed dying at them with an expression more of pity than regret. They would never cleanse themselves of the shame of it.

Levin felt someone tapping him on the shoulder. He jumped up and shrieked. Then he turned to see that it was Marla. His heart was thumping in fear, or, more likely, fury—for how could she dare to tap the shoulder of a man under the threat of death? She couldn't, of course, have known that he had been deeply immersed in threat thinking—but that hardly excused it.

"What is it!" Levin demanded, poisonously. Aware that he had shrieked when she tapped him, he tried to say it in a somewhat shrieking tone, planning to shade his subsequent comments by slight degrees away from shrieking toward regular talking, so that it would seem to her, in retrospect, as if the initial shriek might have been imagined. To his calibrated shrieking tone and his poison, he added a slight shaking of his head in outraged disbelief. But Marla—in her flowery dress which seemed chosen as though to convey her utter allergy to subtlety of any kind—would not have discerned the message of even an overt head-shake, let alone a masterpiece of nuance such as Levin's.

It crossed his mind that she might have come to apologize for her inability to understand the threat, in which case he was ready to forgive her instantly.

She was asking him to sign up to bring something for Adderley's retirement party the following week. She thrust before his face a clipboard with a sign-up sheet, written in impeccable bright-pink cursive script, with a list of items next to which his colleagues had already put their names. The only item that had not been claimed was napkins. Hooked onto the clipboard was a plastic pen shaped like a lobster.

"So it's only napkins left?" Levin said.

"Yes," Marla said.

"Then why did you ask me what I wanted to sign up for? Why didn't you just tell me I had to do napkins?"

Marla shrugged.

So now he had to get napkins—in the midst of death-threat business. First death threats, now sign-up sheets. Where would it end? He buried his face in his hands and let out an animalistic moan. Then he opened his fingers to see that Marla was still standing there, expressionless, waiting patiently for him to finish his moaning.

He touched the lobster pen; then, thinking better of it, in a motion of controlled fury he opened his drawer to retrieve his own silver ballpoint pen, and wrote his name in the napkins slot.

No force in the world could compel him to use a lobster pen.

5

AT HOME THAT NIGHT, AFTER DROPPING OFF A FEW things for Mrs. Cohen at her door—he had been planning to go in and sit with her again; the threat had so energized him that he had thought he would be up to it, but after the frustrations of the day he could not face it after all—and after cleaning up Mildred's vomit piles, he searched the internet for the other Melvin Levins without any élan, doing it merely as a duty, even checking the clock a few times as though there were a certain interval required for this activity which he could hope to make pass quickly.

He came upon a new article by the geologist and, scrolling quickly through it, determined that it didn't represent any great discovery—but all the same, it irked him. There were three co-authors listed, each with their sparkling little PhDs tacked on. And Levin imagined that if the geologist were to receive a death threat, these others—true colleagues, with whom the geologist had slaved through long hours of rock research, and shared many post-research drinks along with rock-related jokes at fine academic-flavored establishments—would rally around him with the utmost respect, sympathy, and awe. *His* threat would be ogled with scientific precision.

Levin scowled at the new article, letting all the day's accumulated poison into the scowl—but rather than disperse the poison, the scowl seemed only to augment it. Even scowls, in his current state, had been ruined.

His back was aching worse than it had in days, and, as if on cue, the wailer started up outside. Her wails now seemed the expression of the world's derision of him.

All the problems that he thought had receded permanently behind the blinding brightness of the threat's menace now came back more vividly than ever, and the threat, rather than representing the invitation to transcend all those petty problems—to step into the higher role that had been his due since birth—was now merely the final huge predicament that bound all the others together into an insuperable trap which Levin's struggles would only close more tightly around him.

He closed his eyes, hoping to strengthen himself with a short respite of oblivion.

When he opened them, he caught sight of something curious: among the mail, which he had thrown unthinkingly into a haphazard pile at the back of his desk, a small package was sticking out that, in its brown paper wrapping tied with red string, struck Levin as unusual.

Could he really have tossed the mail aside with such oblivious haste? Had he been, in the haze of his frustration, so unaware as to have taken it upstairs without even really looking at it—now, of all times?

A feeling of delicious foreboding came over him.

He crept up to the package, took it in his hands, and held it high in the air, as though it were some kind of offering. There was no question about it: it was addressed to Levin in the same hand in which the threat had been.

He wanted first to imbibe the package's very essence, and then to open it with methodical care, one flap at a time, taking note of every precious detail. But once he advanced beyond that thrilling thought, and came to the business of actually imbibing the essence, he was unsure how to do so. He turned the package over, taking in its various angles with furrowed-browed attention, sniff-ing it once or twice.

Then he tore it open with ravenous greed.

A set of half a dozen wallet-size photos tumbled out, and Levin saw, with a rush of excitement, that they were of him. It was a se-ries of black-and-white snapshots that seemed to have been taken surreptitiously from a distance, using a zoom lens, as he had gone about his day.

So now there were snapshots.

He closed his eyes and allowed a blissful smile to come over his face. And he kept the smile there while a new wave of anxiety buffeted him—for he was not immune to the strange, shocking waves of anxiety that the death threat occasioned; the thought that he was going to be killed would still assault him with its re-ality from time to time, and the chest melting and leg manglings would follow in obedient formation—only now these waves were accompanied by something new, an uncanny vibration that went through his body and that lent to the dominant feeling of panic a faint aura of something close to pleasure. How many varieties of panic there were! How many gradations of mortal fear!

Once the anxiety had dissipated, he was overcome by excite-ment. The snapshots that had been granted to him were almost too powerful a weapon. How his colleagues would flush with terror and awe when they saw them, and then rush to apologize, through the suffocation of their shame. "I didn't know there'd be snapshots," Marla would say, unable to believe that she had brought up her brother-in-law's absurd spat. Levin, for his part, would hold up his hands in magnanimous absolution of them all, in acknowledgment of their inferior understanding, and also—he could admit freely—of his own complicity in bringing upon them something for which they were not ready.

Even Meldon—who would not have to be shown the snapshots

directly; word would filter to him in the course of things—would likely make a special point of coming by Levin's cubicle in order to apologize for his callous unconcern: "Look . . . the snapshots change things, that much is clear . . ."

It took all his effort not to rush to the office at once. Even though it was late, he could probably still catch a couple of stragglers and have them do some ogling of the snapshots. If he did catch even one straggler, it might easily set off a rumor that would spread overnight—and who knows what outlandish speculations he would have to tamp down in the morning, or, if he were feeling particularly devilish, encourage with a sly wink!

But he was able to hold himself back and content himself with allowing his excitement to wash over him, placing his hand over his mouth as if to underscore his astonishment at the snapshots— though there was an element, too, of covering a naughty laugh, as if he expected one to break through at any moment.

When he had finished with his mouth-covering, he felt calm enough to take a closer look at the shots.

There were a few problems. In the first snapshot, which showed him entering his apartment building, his bald spot was visible, and, Levin felt, somewhat exaggerated by some combination of the camera angle and the lighting (his head was right next to one of the door lanterns). Also, he was posed awkwardly, half-bending—perhaps after picking something up he had dropped—in such a way as to make it appear as if he had gained a lot of weight. Levin frowned. Presumably the threatener was choosing from a lot of options, a ream of surreptitious shots that allowed flexibility in the choice of which ones to present. Why choose this one?

But, he then thought with a smile, this was all part of the threatener's wiles. Did Levin expect his sworn enemy—the man bent on killing him—to collaborate in assembling a glamor portfolio? Perhaps he also expected him to send a makeup artist and set up lighting equipment?

Levin chuckled aloud at the thought.

He then did what any self-respecting recipient of death-threat photos ought to do without making a fuss about it: he simply placed the unsatisfactory photo in a drawer and eyed the remaining collection, still considerable, with satisfaction. He felt like the commander of a huge, powerful army who can idle whole battalions without decreasing the enemy's fear even a jot.

The next photo, too, he soon set aside. It showed him leaving a pharmacy, and because not all his purchases could fit into his bag, he had been forced to carry in his other hand a roll of paper towels, causing him to appear rather undignified.

Another photo, zoomed in through the front window of a bakery, had caught a moment of weakness in which Levin had purchased two slices of cake. This one, too, he set aside. In another, he realized with a start, his shirt was misbuttoned.

Two more photos had to be eliminated for bald-spot reasons.

He soon realized, with chagrin, that he had eliminated all but a single photo, which was completely blurred.

With some trepidation, Levin pulled the whole pile back from the drawer in which it had been stowed. He stared at it in vexation. He shifted the photos around on the desk for long minutes, moving one and then another beneath the light of his banker's lamp, taking some small consolatory pleasure in the sweeping sound of the sleek shots as they zipped over his desk beneath his fingertips, until he finally settled on the pharmacy shot and one of the bald-spot shots in which his proximity to an enormously fat old man seemed to mitigate some of Levin's own defects by comparison.

Satisfied, he turned to the rest of the contents of the package. A white rag and a baseball card tumbled out of it, along with a note. Levin picked up the rag and examined it. It was a bit dirty, with dark smudges in places, and in one corner the letter R had been written in red ink. The baseball card was of Greg Maddux.

Levin was once again frowning. He was not, in principle, against a collection of strange items being part of the threat. Collections of strange items could produce a mysterious and suggestive aura of great deliciousness. But was this aura delicious? For one thing, two items did not really constitute a "collection." Also, something about the items seemed not quite right. Levin couldn't put his finger on it—but then he was not steeped in the mechanics of death threats, nor should that be expected of him. In time, of course, such expertise would accrue; but for now he was merely a person of a certain considerable degree of acuity who had, of necessity, become interested in the subject of death threats—and even in that modest capacity he could immediately see that a baseball card and a rag with a letter had something amateurish about them.

Shouldn't he have been sent something more overtly mysterious? Rusty keys? An old map? Even a skull, or a non-skull bone . . . Once again he was forced to confront the possibility that he was dealing with a threatener of the third or even fourth rank. Could Levin be expected to bring these items before a committee of respectable people evaluating death threats—should such a committee ever be formed—without embarrassment? He sighed.

But then the snapshots had indicated such professionalism! Why they should be accompanied by inadequate items was simply puzzling . . .

Yes, puzzling . . . a puzzle . . . a downright puzzle . . .

And Levin suddenly grinned. For he saw what the threatener had assembled here: a puzzle.

Yes! It was *he*, not the threatener, who was the amateur—the philistine pining for a threat full of clichés. A skull and a bone! He was tempted to laugh at loud at his own error.

After all, you can't expect all the elements of a death threat to open themselves up to interpretation in an instant, like a game intended for children! Death-threat artifacts were things meant to be puzzled over for a long time—for weeks, months, or perhaps even longer—and there was always the possibility that a complete answer would never emerge, that even after you were killed (though Levin, at moments such as this, when his mind was airy with the difficult pleasure of unraveling the threat, had no doubt he would not be killed but would defeat it), the authorities would have to say, "There were certain aspects of the threat that we will never understand . . . for example, the baseball card."

Levin felt a shiver of excitement. Beneath the excitement, there was, too, a sense of abashedness, as though he ought to nod to the threatener in apology for having doubted him.

He looked again at the rag and the baseball card, this time with the proper appreciation for their significance. No doubt the puzzle was an extraordinarily difficult one—but solvable all the same. After all, it had been made for Levin, was meant for him alone, and it was now his fate that it should absorb his attention for long weeks or possibly even years. He would weary himself with it. It was a grave, profound task worthy of him and worthy of the threat itself.

Yes, it would take years to tease out the metaphorical significance of the puzzle—and yet it would be good to have a few metaphors to start with, in case anyone asked.

He pulled his notebook in front of him, closed his eyes, and concentrated with all his might on coming up with some metaphors. Complex, suggestive images flitted through his mind with dizzying speed. He saw now the baseball card, now the rag, each growing and transforming into other potentialities—the card becoming a tree, under which a grave (his? the threatener's?) took its shade; saw the R on the rag expand and contract, and transform into other letters, as though suggesting the limitless words it might stand for. He remained in this state for several minutes. He had the sense that all his brainpower was being drawn upon in the interest of dealing with the threat, a feeling of indescribable satisfaction. Whereas before he had dithered—drawing up ineffectual lists of implausible suspects, wasting his energy on thoughts of the rubes in the office and how they were taking it—now he was harnessing every ounce of potential within him in the service of defeating the threat.

Putting these images into words was another matter, one that could be safely left to another day. The vital breakthrough was in having accessed the reservoir of imagery at the deepest level of his consciousness, that whirl of symbolic thought that he felt sure would not only unlock the puzzle but penetrate to the *essence* of the threat. He could certainly revisit this reservoir later, when he had more energy. For now, he simply wrote "metaphors" on his to-do list, and turned back to the marvelous threat items.

He felt he was coming to know his adversary better and better. There was, in this cat-and-mouse game, a certain rapport developing between them—perhaps even, in a way that an unthreatened person would not be able to understand, a certain mutual respect. By giving the threatener the benefit of the doubt and interpreting the threat items in their most mysterious light, Levin had extended a certain respect to him, and he felt that that respect would certainly be paid in return—had already been paid, in fact, since the very existence of the snapshots, so arduously obtained, was itself a sign of respect.

He closed his eyes and once again saw the threatener in his lair—a lair which, he now realized, was not the dark and mahogany-paneled chamber of espionage he had first envisioned but instead must be sleek, metallic, glinting, lit very well in order to maximize the glinting, and buzzing with technological wizardry.

This was a place from which snapshots originated! It was full of the finest digital photographic equipment and telescopes—and since Levin lacked the knowledge of what cutting-edge telescopes looked like, he simply imagined them to be incredibly long and thin, but strong as diamond.

He had almost forgotten that there was a new note. He felt a rush of anticipation as though discovering one last overlooked Christmas present in the corner. The note was written in red ink, in the same girlish hand in which the original threat had been. It read:

> I'm watching you and before long your toast. I coud care less. Don't even think about making any sudden

And that was all. It simply broke off, mid-sentence.

Obviously the threatener had forgotten to finish the note.

He turned it over; the back was blank. He grabbed the package and looked through it for a hidden scrap, then began to paw with increasingly frantic movements around the table, pushing aside papers, picking up books to look under them—until, with sudden decision, he stopped.

No. No: he was not going to dispense with his good spirits so quickly. He was lapsing into a pre-threatened state of mind, one of primitive hysteria. He need not do that now: he would remain calm and impassive.

He took a deep breath. So what if the threatener had not finished the note? It was something that could happen to anyone. Were threateners of death immune to distraction? There were probably a million demands coming at them from all sides at all times. And anyway this was a threatener whose mind had been on more important things, which he had completed perfectly well . . .

On . . . snapshots . . .

He let the word permeate his body like a narcotic.

Levin was once again enchanted. He set aside the uncompleted note without a further glance at it.

In his ebullience, he was almost sorry that he had already cleaned Mildred's vomit piles so that he could not now do so with joyful ease. He decided to go for a stroll and pick up some dinner. On his way out of the apartment, Mildred eyed him. Levin stared back at her, smiling broadly and extending his hands in a gesture of generosity—with animals you don't need to be as careful with expressions—as if to reassure the cat that he would be very glad to clean up any additional vomit, that she should look upon this as an opportunity to enjoy complete freedom to vomit.

But Mildred merely stared back with steely reserve—as though to say that she knew as well as a person that to make Levin clean vomit now was a profanity that should be avoided when not absolutely necessary.

6

THE AIR WAS CRISP, AND AS THE SUN WENT DOWN THE ruddy shadowing of the streets was pleasing to Levin. Earlier he had regretted the clearness of the day, wishing for a return of the rain that could once again lend his death threat the befogged, mysterious surroundings it demanded. But he saw now how short-sighted that had been. The clement weather as a background for the death threat had a charm of its own, the lengthening shadows lending their own air of mystery to things as effectively as the mist-filled air had done the night before. He had not anticipated what pleasures ruddy shadowings could bring. How many colorations a death threat could take on in different weathers, different climes! Would he have time to discover them all, to travel the world and experience a death threat in Rome and Venice, the Far East, even at sea? Probably his death-threat concerns would keep him far too busy for such peregrinations. But it was permissible to dream . . .

His smile, his mien and bearing—how right he had been to place such importance on these things! For there were now snapshots—he kept repeating the phrase to himself as he walked— and although they had been taken before he had developed his death-threat bearing, still they were a testament to how important it was, since for all he knew the threatener could be taking more photos of him at this very instant . . .

And it was a sign of how far Levin had come that, though he recognized the immense importance of how he was carrying himself as he walked, he barely once checked his reflection in a storefront window.

With little hesitation, he headed straight for the fancy restaurant. The stunning coat-check woman was wearing a polka-dotted dress that he was not expecting, but without letting that throw him off, he placed his coat on the counter before her with meticulous neatness and a solemn bow of the head. Here was a coat, he seemed to indicate, that had been in surreptitious photos (this particular coat wasn't in any of the photos, but that was something she couldn't have known). She took up the coat and began her graceful process. And if he should allow one of the snapshots to "slip" out onto the counter, by accident . . . ?

He moved away from the coat-check area quickly, his face hot with terror at what he might be capable of.

The maître d' told him they had no available tables. For a moment Levin panicked. He had already checked his coat! He considered bolting for the exit: he could put an emergency in his eyes and run away, and certainly it could be justified later as part of death-threat business.

But the maître d' was apologetic and embarrassed in the ideal amounts, and Levin understood that these kinds of situations were unavoidable, that in the places where life-and-death matters were discussed, tables were in high demand, and sometimes even the most important men in the world would have to be turned away. He shrugged magnanimously.

He began to walk toward the coat check. The coat-check woman had—virtuosa that she was—placed his coat on the counter; already no number was needed between them, nor were explanations about a lack of tables.

On the other hand, it would be good to say *something*; he should smooth things over, if only with a joke . . .

He was becoming frightened. He had no plan, and was now only steps away from the window.

Then he noticed that the coat-check woman was, confusingly, putting on one of the coats herself. It seemed a kind of absurdist performance art; then for an insane moment it crossed his mind that his being denied a table had driven her to resign. But quickly he saw that she was simply done with her shift, and was being replaced by a lanky old gentleman with huge fists who was systematically laying a number of personal items on the counter as though he were preparing not to attend the coat check but to live there.

So, if he had waited a few moments, he could have avoided her ever knowing about this table mix-up . . . What awful timing!

But it was too late, she had seen him and laid out his coat, was in fact practically face to face with him now, having left the coat check and started walking to the door; it seemed they might almost bump into one another . . . His heart was pounding . . .

He wanted to make a joke about how his schedule had shifted unexpectedly, but as he was trying to locate the words for it, he instead spoke suddenly, without thought.

"May I walk with you?" he said.

He was stunned. He could not believe that he had said it. He could feel the blood rushing to his cheeks and was almost worried that they would burst before she could respond.

"Sure," she said.

The next moments transpired without his understanding how. He felt as though he were observing rather than controlling his own body. Somehow he found himself outside—and, beside him, the coat-check woman.

It was true: he was now walking side by side with the coat-check woman. Yes, it was happening, though it seemed impossible; he was vibrating with a strange, distracting energy, and everything seemed distant, fog-covered. *Sure*, she had said, *sure*... Had she? Is that what had happened?

Yes. Of course she had said "sure." Why shouldn't she? He was a man under the threat of death, after all—a man who is the subject of snapshots! And all his fascinating troubles were exuded by the manner and bearing that he had perfected: she sensed them, of course. And when such a man offers to walk, the only thing to do is to say "sure," to say it quickly!

But as sound as he knew this reasoning to be, he could not really believe in it; his hands were shaking, and—though to make a far-from-minor alteration to his death-threat gait now, of all times, when it was being put to its greatest test, was in some ways reckless—he had no choice but to put them in his pockets.

He admonished himself to calm down. "You are a man in snapshots!" he scolded himself sharply.

Then he spoke aloud: "A lovely evening."

He tensed all his muscles, as though awaiting a blow from a person he had just recklessly insulted.

"Yes," she said, smiling.

"Are you on your way home now?"

"No, I'm meeting a friend."

He did not know how he was finding these perfect questions; some external being was as though guiding him, speaking through him. And she, for her part, was answering with perfect naturalness. Obviously she found nothing wanting in the questions, or in the situation more broadly.

And he realized, gaining confidence, that he was not only maintaining his fine gait and bearing amid the surreal circumstances—he was doing so spectacularly. Certainly no part of her was thinking, "How could I be walking with a person of this gait?"

He removed his hands from his pockets. "Do you live in this neighborhood?"

Not only did she tell him that she did not, but she actually volunteered the neighborhood where she did live. And then she spoke, totally without prompting, of her roommate, who—he was astonished at the revelation—annoyed her. Nor was that all: she then added that she was—secretly: the roommate did not even know it—considering moving out, to the point of having even browsed listings.

What was prompting these confessions?

"Have you worked at the restaurant long?"

"About two years."

"Ah, I see, two years . . ." Now he was in full possession of his faculties—now he had at his disposal the full range of his sparkling wit! What was prompting the confessions was he himself, his aura, his being. He was a man under the threat of death, a man in snapshots, walking down the street with a beautiful young woman, and he felt it, he felt it in every fiber of his body. "Two years," he said again. And now he would cap it off with an unforgettable *bon mot* . . .

But she spoke again before he could—so great was her comfort with the seemliness of their walking. "It's a way to support myself while I work on my passion," she said.

He glanced at her; with two of her fingers, she was smoothing back a lock of hair that had fallen over her eyes.

He was full of daring now. "You want to be a performer," he said.

"How did you know?"

He beamed. He knew it was wrong, knew it was a flagrantly uncalibrated smile—and he looked downward bashfully, to keep it from her as much as possible—but he could not help it, he was too delighted. He was about to explain how he knew, was on the point of saying, "Why, from your manner with the coats, of course!"—but then he realized that this would be a false step, that he must be laconic, mysterious, must exude his wisdom from his manner and bearing and *only* from them.

And they walked on in silence for several moments, he doing his best to exude knowingness and wisdom—trying to make it shine through his eyes, lifting his eyebrows a couple of times to help—though it was difficult to exude only knowingness while a thrilling joy was coursing through him.

Then he said, "Are you by any chance . . . a dancer?"

"An actor."

"Ah," he said quietly.

They lapsed once again into silence.

And then, before he knew it, she had reached her destination, a coffee shop. They stood facing each other. He nodded deeply, to ratify the new intimacy between them; and she, once again, brushed back her hair with two fingers. That would have been enough, of course—but then she unleashed a smile that nearly knocked him backward. This was not the smile of coat-sorting! No, it was the smile of her everyday joys—the smile that she bared to the men and women who populated the most intimate, sacred premises of her life.

And then she was gone.

He stood for a while without moving. He was vibrating with the thrill of having done something so bold. It was an uncomfortable feeling. The vibrations carried an excess of energy, and he felt a bit like he had had ten cups of coffee. He wanted to run around in maniacal circles, screaming, but he knew with sober resignation that his days of maniacal running were over now, even if he were to do that running without any screams.

He had asked to walk with the coat-check woman—and they had done so; they had walked together. And later, perhaps, he would mention it offhand to someone; someone would point out the coat-check woman and he would say, almost absent-mindedly,

"I walked with her . . ."—as though these kinds of things were, for him, barely worth mentioning.

When he reached his apartment, he was still vibrating. In the middle of the living room he jumped up and down several times to try to dissipate some of the energy, before stopping suddenly as he recalled his complaining downstairs neighbor. He looked downward with a fearful expression on his face and crouched slowly toward the floor, as though he could retroactively cancel at least some of the jumping by this opposite movement. He remained crouched for several minutes. Then he remembered that he, a man under the threat of death, had nothing to fear from the complaining of a neighbor.

And he jumped a couple more times, with less energy and more quietly, but they were jumps all the same; no one could dispute it.

For he was coming to understand that to be a man under the threat of death means more than mere miens and bearings: it also means actions. A mien and bearing—no matter how fabulous— are *in and of themselves* empty, unless and until they are lent substance by action. He had asked the coat-check woman to walk, and just look at all that had followed from that incredible boldness, all that he had learned about her—that she was an actor, that she lived on the fourth floor and that the stairs were steep, that she browsed listings, that her roommate's name was Viola . . . that Viola left dirty coffee mugs everywhere . . .

He blushed to recall these disclosures.

And there was something else he knew now, too: that she brushed back her hair with two fingers . . .

He was in possession of these marvelous facts solely because of his outrageous boldness—because of the insane act of daring that, days before, would have been unthinkable.

And just think, without it he would hardly know her at all.

One must act! One must speak out in the elevator with the

lawyers! One must—he blushed again to recall it, but rebuffed the blush with a determined glare—ask coat-check women to go on walks, and then endure the resulting discomfort of one's boldness as though it were nothing!

His gaze caught the latest note from the threatener, which he had set aside before. He walked up to it and read it again, this time with renewed strength and courage. As he read, he tightened his face into a menacing scowl in order to reinforce his strength against the offense that the note leveled at him, with its solecisms and its awful trailing off:

I'm watching you and before long your toast. I coud care less. Don't even think about making any sudden

He noticed that beside the note was a red pen that he had left there by pure happenstance. The sight almost alarmed him. With mounting anxiety, his gaze moved from the red pen to the red ink in which the note was written, and then back again to the pen, which had been placed beside it almost as though to guide him. Yes—it was a sign. Was he going to be the man of action that he had so confidently proclaimed it his destiny to be? Or was he to remain only a man who—though called to the higher plane, and though inhabiting it with some of the outward motions and superficial trappings—clings only to thoughts and intentions and leaves his aspirations unfulfilled?

Terrified now, he stared at the pen, knowing that in some sense it represented a ratification of his destiny—a destiny that made him shudder with fear but that he also knew, with a certain undeniable elation, he must fulfill.

Then he remembered that this particular pen, though its cap was red, actually had black ink. With a quick and almost violent motion he opened a drawer and rifled through it for a red pen, which he placed on the desk where the misleading black pen had been. Then he moved back and reattained his position of frightened consideration, staring at the red pen, which was becoming an irresistible temptation.

Mildred had entered the room and was looking intently at him, as though she too understood the moment's importance. Levin felt as though he represented, before the cat, the whole of the human race.

Trembling, he took the pen and held it above the note. He was shaking so much as he brought the pen downward that twice he had to abort at the last second, jerking it away.

But finally he forced it down, and with swift strokes made the "your" into a "you're," added an "l" to the "coud"—the way the letter slotted in with perfect neatness in its tiny place gave Levin an immense boost of confidence—and then, at the end, where it trailed off with: "Don't even think about making any sudden," he added the word "moves."

He stared at what he had done. He was no longer trembling. The impeccable success of his corrections—the daring risk overcome—had given him a feeling of thrilled delight. He was becoming more and more accustomed to the feeling that marked the aftermaths of his boldnesses—and beginning to enjoy it.

And with great swiftness—as though the length of time he took to make any alteration would somehow show on the page—he wrote, at the end of the note, "Though you are proving a more worthy adversary than anyone here expected, we are making the appropriate adjustments."

Levin grinned. He was intoxicated by having acted with such daring.

He turned to look at the expectant cat, and his tremendously good spirits were not diminished by the fact that she had walked away. It was not difficult for Levin to imagine that she had done so only a moment before, after witnessing his boldness.

7

EVIN'S GOOD SPIRITS WERE INTACT THE NEXT MORN-
ing. His panic on awakening lasted an astonishingly short
time—he even managed to finish breakfast before the manglings
were fully dissipated, letting them course through him one after
another as he munched his scone—and he was out the door with
time to spare, even after spending a long time packing the original
threat, the new note, the snapshots, the rag, and the baseball card
into a fine small leather briefcase which he had inherited from a
grandfather and never used. The fact that he finally had a proper
use for this briefcase delighted him. He placed the threat and the
snapshots in separate manila folders, wrapped the baseball card in
bubble wrap, and put it all into the valise along with munificent
amounts of tissue paper, wadded up and jammed throughout to
prevent any shifting en route.

In the office he walked to his cubicle with unfettered confidence. He would be quite content not to show the new threat
items to anyone, and had brought them to work mainly as a precaution against a burglary in his apartment, and, secondarily, as
a secret source of strength, a kind of bulwark against the terrible
suffering that men under the threat of death must bear in dignified silence. Certainly they would remain concealed in his fine valise, unmentioned.

Oh, he could drop a hint or two. Over the course of the day,
he could let slip a remark that one of the more clever among them
might pick up on, perhaps only months later. "Well, I'm not

exactly ready to be photographed right *now*, am I?" Levin could say, when momentarily in some comically awkward position—if he spilled coffee, for example. But to spill it naturally would require some practice . . .

No, he was perfectly content to sit in silence with the knowledge of the amazing escalation the threat had undertaken—to let his uncultivated colleagues cluster around Flemingson and ask if there were updates on the mugging, to offer up to him their saccharine porridge of unsophisticated sympathy, while Levin remained apart, reflecting on the profoundness of his own predicament in the solitude that was its only appropriate setting.

Leonard, the mustachioed enthusiast, approached Levin. He was holding something that for a brief and terrifying moment Levin thought was a threat of his own. But Levin quickly saw, laughing at his own jumpiness, that it was merely an ordinary bit of office work that Leonard had just retrieved from the printer.

"Any developments with the threat?" Leonard asked.

He was standing in a pose of great enthusiasm, in a very red plaid which he seemed to have selected for the occasion, his cheeks flushing deeply.

Levin was greatly touched by Leonard's curiosity. The inappropriateness of the threat as a subject for Leonard's enthusiasm was still a fact, one that couldn't simply be waved away, but its coloration had somehow changed. Now Leonard's enthusiasm for the threat seemed less a crass and unforgivable presumption than a pathetic but nevertheless flattering gesture. Levin felt as though a child had approached him holding a complicated mathematics textbook he'd found, begging to be taught the subject that was immeasurably beyond his comprehension.

The feeling of being a wizened, generous teacher that resulted from this image was impossible for Levin to resist. He wanted to throw his arms outward and gesture everyone to gather round so that he could bestow a lesson. It took all his strength to suppress the urge to say, "Gather round," and he could not fully suppress the accompanying urge to do some arm-waving. Then he spilled all the new threat items onto the desk in a gesture of controlled insanity.

The sound produced by this spilling—a bit of extravagance with which Levin had shocked himself (and the sight of the items on the desk produced a secondary shock: how could these almost sacred things be simply lying there, exposed!)—had neatly accomplished Levin's purpose. All around the office, heads were popping up from the petty drivel in which they had been immersed; Marla was already making her way over. And Levin realized at once how easy it was to form a tableau. Objects is all it takes—material things. Like dogs with shiny toys . . .

"Is this about the thingie?" Marla asked.

"It's about the *threat*," Levin said, with firmness not unleavened by a certain tenderness.

"Oh," Marla said. Levin looked at her and filled his eyes with generous indulgence, of the kind you bestow on a pupil whose progress in the face of real learning challenges has made you proud.

A couple of other people—newcomers to the threat—came as well. "He's got a thingie," Marla said.

"A threat," Levin said. Then he spoke rapidly: "I've been threatened with death by an anonymous note and now the threatener has sent a new collection of items including snapshots." As he spoke, he carefully averted his eyes from the newcomers, as if to issue a slight reprimand for their not knowing about the threat.

"The items are mysterious," Levin went on once everyone was settled. "No doubt they were selected carefully in order to send a message of some kind. The question is, of course, what that message is. I already have some ideas, but I don't feel it would be appropriate to discuss them here."

It was to be his finest hour. He felt that he had penetrated to a new, deeper understanding of his life as a man under the threat of death—one who inhabits the higher plane of existence, of course, and who indulges the occasional good-natured laugh at those toiling beneath him, but who also is able to converse with those lower people, to get down into their world and with a kind of Christlike humility establish meaningful communication with them; to teach them and—it was even possible—to learn something from them in turn.

"It's a rag," said Leonard.

"That's right. A rag," said Levin, raising his eyebrows in a couple of little spasms meant to hint that he knew much more than he was letting on. He waited for Leonard to find the letter R.

"It has the letter R on it," said Leonard. Levin only shrugged.

"It must mean something," said Leonard. His enthusiasm face was coming over him—his cheeks flushing more deeply with the determination to find out what this all meant.

"There's also this," Levin said, pushing the baseball card toward the enthusiast.

"A baseball card . . ." Leonard said, becoming lost in his enthusiasm. "Greg Maddux. He may be trying to convey something about himself. Perhaps the initials G.M. are significant . . ."

Levin smiled a condescending smile. "Yes, it's possible . . ."

"Or it could be more symbolic," Leonard said.

Levin turned to Marla. "I suppose your brother-in-law never received mysterious items."

And all she could do was shake her head, no doubt in embarrassment at the suggestion of such a thing.

Levin was now so confident in the power of the threat that he even looked around for Dennis, the skeptic, to see if he could be waved over—let him try his skepticism against these items!

Leonard's flush of enthusiasm had reached a very deep shade

of red, delighting Levin. "This is going to be a tough one to solve, there's no doubt about that," he said.

"We may *never* solve it," Levin said proudly.

That evening, he treated himself to a well-deserved respite. The threat had been occupying his mind with such unremitting intensity that a great fatigue had built up within him without his noticing. He allowed himself to relax in front of the television—though even now he found, not without satisfaction, that his thoughts turned again and again to the threat. A man under the threat of death never truly rests, and even leisure time is for him only another form of the ceaseless toil by which his life is bound and constrained.

No doubt the same was true of the threatener, who, in his lair—which Levin now imagined to be spare and minimalist, a sinister work of modernist art—probably kept a notebook handy even when he relaxed, in case a new idea for how to kill Levin occurred to him.

At one point, Levin's attention was arrested by something on the TV. It was a mystery show or movie that he had come across only a moment before. A blond woman was opening a package and unwrapping something that was wadded up with layers of newspaper. She peeled them back, layer after layer, to reveal a blood-engorged severed toe. The woman dropped the toe and then screamed in terror, her eyes bulging in shock.

Levin sat upright. He was entranced. To be sent a severed toe in a package! It was an unforgettable image, and so was the look of terror in the woman's eyes as the toe came into view. Would his own threatener proceed to such spectacular tactics? Such a thing couldn't be ruled out—not after snapshots had been sent.

He turned off the TV in order to focus his attention fully on this thrilling new aspect of the threat. Its future appeared as an endless vista of potential terrors which were only now beginning to occur to him. The vigilance necessary to counteract such things—and Levin thought with a smirk that the blond woman, with her terrified shriek, knew nothing of threats, even as the memory of that wide-eyed shriek thrilled him in a deep part of himself—was a new challenge, one he would have to meet.

He went to his desk in order to contemplate the threat more.

His mind was flooded with images—not only of severed toes and screaming blondes, but of other macabre things that might be sent in order to menace someone: dead animals, or parts of animals; bones; personal items that had been ingeniously purloined from Levin's intimate pockets without his being aware, such as his library card. The toe, too, kept coming back in different guises— wrapped up more and more elaborately, or hidden in surprising places around his apartment.

He had, in short, become a fount of ideas for how the threat could be made to sparkle with terror. He had the strange impulse to write these ideas down, as though he himself were planning to threaten someone in the future. Smiling at the silliness of this notion, he got up and merely jotted down a few words in his notebook for each idea.

The sight of the words in his notebook gave him a feeling of great accomplishment.

He rewarded himself by dining at the fancy restaurant. And though he was disappointed that the coat-check woman was not on duty—instead, it was the man with fists; who can say what would have happened otherwise, what new disclosures might have come, perhaps even a second walk!—still, it was a pleasure; he was seated and dined without incident, immersed as he was in the satisfaction of his productive work of the evening.

As he was walking home, his phone rang.

The screen showed an unidentified caller. His heart sped up.

He answered the call and, with his hand that he now realized was shaking violently, did his best to press the phone against his ear. "Hello?" he stammered.

A voice said: "Is this Melvin Levin?"

A tightness took hold of Levin's chest. He could barely breathe.

"Is this . . . the threatener?"

"Yes," the voice said.

The tightness in Levin's chest was obliterated by an explosion of anxiety such as he had never experienced—as though the tightness had been storing up energy in readiness.

But beneath the layers of unbelievable panic, he could detect, also, a hint of excitement—for he was now a man facing the threat of death, on the phone with the very man who wished to kill him.

"Hello," Levin said again, his voice shaking.

"Hello," the threatener said.

Steadying himself against a mailbox, he was able to calm himself very quickly. How expert he had become at panicking! The corrosive poison continued to course through his chest, more sporadically, but not to any degree that would distract him from the all-important test that had suddenly been thrust before him.

And he leaned against the mailbox at a suave angle, resting his elbow on it and relaxing his body into a posture of parlor-room nonchalance, as though the mailbox were a decorative object in his own house. For he was now ready to converse with the threatener as his worthy foe, two equals locked in battle.

Then he realized, with some alarm, that there was silence on the line, and must have been for some time.

"Hello?" Levin said, for a third time.

"Yes," said the threatener.

"Can you hear me all right?"

"Yes, I can hear you."

There was another silence.

"Well, did you want to . . . talk about the threat?" Levin said.
"Yes."

A tall man holding a huge stack of envelopes was glaring at Levin, who it turned out was blocking the opening of the mailbox. Levin moved aside, somewhat perturbed by the man's gruff annoyance—as though this mailbox were the only one for miles—and then thought that it was actually serendipitous that he had been interrupted in this way, for mailbox leanings weren't really right for a threat call. The thing to do was to walk, and walk rapidly—to dart among the masses as he engaged in the dangerous conversational *pas de deux* with his sworn nemesis that was now to commence!

"Who are you?" Levin said, pleased with having thought of this important question.

"I'm your worst nightmare."

"I see."

"Just a minute," the threatener said.

"Okay."

And now as Levin walked, he felt himself charged with a new kind of aliveness. He was handling the call magnificently. Here he was—a man under the threat of death, on the phone with his threatener, speeding through busy streets! And as he passed people, he thought to himself, "If they only knew what was going on in front of them—while they talk about how much asparagus to get for dinner!"

For at any moment he would continue the high-stakes *pas de deux* in which he was now engaged with the man bent on his destruction.

On the line he could hear a strange sound—a kind of clacking with a wetness underlying it, as though the threatener were rapping a ruler against a pile of soaked papers.

"Are you there?" Levin said. But only the clacking continued.

Finally the threatener said, "I'm back."

"Hello," Levin said again. And after another silence, he added, "You said you wanted to talk about the threat."

Levin now had a slightly unpleasant sensation. He could not help but feel as though he were drawing conversation out of a shy child with great effort. And there was something else that was adding to his slight feeling of deflatedness: the threatener's voice was not quite what he had imagined. It was faint—as though he were speaking at some distance from the phone—and, it had to be admitted, wheezy. The wheeziness verged at times, it was true, on gravelliness, and it was possible that he was dealing with a voice whose true gravelly nature was being temporarily concealed by a throat issue that might be resolved (at any moment) with a clearing; but for now the voice had to be characterized—Levin was not going to deny this, not when clear-eyedness was the most crucial thing—as wheezy, and even weak.

"I'm going to slice you open like a package," the threatener said, "and roast you over a fire with your legs first. I'm going to stab your eyes out."

Here, at last, were the threats. Levin was enormously relieved. Fearful, too, no doubt—but he was now able to admit to himself the large extent to which he had, though unjustly, for a moment doubted the threatener's seriousness.

It was not out of the question that the threatener had intentionally conveyed an unreadiness in order to lull Levin into this underestimation of him.

The threatener had paused again, and Levin, unsure whether the two threats he had leveled were the beginning of a longer threat list or constituted the entirety of the threats for today, experienced a new welling-up of anxiety as he considered whether to respond. He opened his mouth, and then cautiously began, "Well—"

But the threatener continued, causing Levin to close his mouth with relief. "I'm going to throw you in a vat of acid. I'm going to saw off your legs and—"

And the threatener broke into a coughing fit. But, coughing or not, these were undeniable threats that would be taken seriously by anyone.

The coughing continued for longer than Levin might have liked, the most intense hacks jagged and irregular enough to make him wince as he listened. It was true that there was nothing very out of place about wincing while on a death-threat call, but Levin nevertheless wished for the coughing fit to pass as quickly as possible.

Finally the threatener recovered. "I'm sorry. Where was I?"

"I think the last one you said was sawing off my legs."

"I'm going to throw you in a vat of acid—"

"No, you said that one," Levin said, a bit disappointed. Then he hastened to add: "Unless you *meant* to repeat it."

"One second," said the threatener. Levin frowned. Another interruption was really unwelcome. Was the threatener working on something else simultaneously? Another threat even? Levin's threat ought to take first priority. Unless there were extraordinary circumstances—Levin was ready to be reasonable about it—but then that ought to be explained up front.

"I'm back."

"Okay."

After another pause, the threatener said, "Well, all right then."

Levin was alarmed. Was the threatener about to end the call? The thought for some reason set Levin reeling again.

Suddenly Levin spoke: "Wait!"

"Yes?" the threatener said.

He had called out without thinking—which was certainly the prerogative, even the obligation, of a man now accustomed to boldnesses such as he was. He had, after all, walked with the coat-check woman. But now he was unsure what to say. There was a nagging sensation that the call was incomplete somehow—that if he were to allow it to end, he would be letting some crucial opportunity slip away. But what?

"I just want to tell you," he began, cautiously, feeling his way, "that I thought the snapshots were first-rate."

And once he had said the words "first-rate," he realized that his voice had shifted, out of nervousness, in such a way that made it sound almost teasing, a tone that Levin immediately realized he should continue. So he repeated the words again, this time in an intentionally teasing tone: "I thought the snapshots were *first-rate*."

Then he went on: "And whatever else you're planning . . ." He slowed down, for here he had reached a critical juncture. "Be it more snapshots . . . Or be it something similar to snapshots, something even more menacing, perhaps . . . No more baseball cards, I expect." He slathered these last words with so much playfulness that he half expected the threatener to break into a laugh.

"What baseball cards?" the threatener said.

"The Greg Maddux card."

"Oh, I've been looking for that."

Levin hardly winced, pressing on: "Well, whatever it is— a skull, something blood-soaked . . . maybe a dead animal . . . well, I don't need to tell you your business as a threatener, of course . . . I just want you to know I'll be ready."

Defiance. That is what had been missing: he ought not let a threatener call pass without showing defiance. And now he had done so.

And, tensing his belly and raising his shoulders so that defiance was coursing out of him in thick currents, he said again: "I'll be ready."

A woman brushing past him—he had slowed down in order to focus on his defiance—caused him to start in fright, and possibly to let out a little yelp. But, yelp or not, it didn't matter: the defiance had been shown successfully and need not be prolonged. It was time to bring things to a close.

A silence was persisting on the line. Levin said: "Well, is that all? Or did you want to threaten more?"

"No, that's all."

"All right. Goodbye."

"Goodbye."

Levin, somewhat winded, sat on a bench, both to catch his breath and to take stock of what had occurred.

All in all, the call had gone rather well. Had it been a *pas de deux*? Yes. There was no question about it: he had engaged, without warning or preparation, in a tense exchange of sallies in which he had, if not come out the winner—he didn't dare to think it—at least achieved a draw.

It was true that the weak and wheezing voice, and the laconic pauses, were things that had to be contended with. It remained a distinct possibility that the threatener's voice was gravelly, of course—but for now that could not be assumed. In the meantime, he had to acknowledge that these things did not seem to fit with his image of the threatener, which had been so meticulously crafted.

And, calling to mind that image—the threatener with his close-cropped hair and fine, dark clothing, the look of spy-like professionalism glinting with menace—he began to make certain adjustments in order to accommodate it to the new information he had just obtained. If he aged the face by about ten years . . . If he refashioned the image not around sleekness, but around a slight manic disorganization . . . wild hair, clothes with some tattering that suggested a menacing zaniness, a dangerous unpredictability . . . but all of it still intimating a force of great control, great subtlety, operating underneath . . . Yes, it was not difficult to square the weakness and wheezing of the voice—and even, Levin thought with a start, the coughing fits!—with this image. Even the spelling mistakes made perfect sense now, all those miscues—far from being evidence of incompetence, they befitted the threatener's mercurial character and only underscored his specific menace!

They would have implications for his lair as well, these alterations—but Levin felt he could responsibly leave lair alterations to another time.

He walked home with airy steps, secure in the knowledge that a new test had been thrust upon him, and that he had, with hardly a hesitation, passed it.

At home, looking at the notebook in which he had jotted the ideas for escalations that the threat might undertake, he was struck by how many had not occurred to him while on the phone with the threatener. Levin scolded himself.

But then, wasn't the threatener hard at work on his own escalation ideas—perhaps at this very moment?

And, grinning, Levin got into bed, imagining the threatener's terrific productivity—hard at work on an escalation that would shock and stun them all, even (and here Levin allowed himself a bit of the unaccountable whimsy that is permitted in dreams) the coat-check woman.

As he fell asleep, he felt humbled, gently castigating himself for the mistakes he had made in his earlier imaginings of the threatener. A little more humility in these matters would not be a bad thing, Levin thought. The feeling of humbling himself was intensely pleasant: he felt as though, as a man on the higher plane of existence, preoccupied with life-and-death concerns, to contemplate one's own humility was like a quaint little vacation.

In truth, he had never been more satisfied with the threat against him, which seemed simultaneously bursting with danger and also a thing that he would surely vanquish—though only after the appropriate struggle.

8

For several days, Levin inhabited the higher plane of existence with a newfound sense of security and ease. He felt that nothing could knock him off of it—for he was now a man under the threat of death who had spoken with his own threatener on the phone, engaged in a tense and fast-paced *pas de deux* with him, danced the dance of death and emerged stronger than ever to tell the tale.

He now walked with effortless confidence, barely ever checking his reflection. On the elevator, he offered the lawyers deep, hearty nods that were met instantaneously with reciprocal nods of their own. And when he did not see them in the lobby, he would linger, pace around, pretend to be checking a certain flier on the wall, in the hope that one of them would come—which sometimes occurred.

He had purchased a few threat accoutrements and arranged them around his cubicle, transforming his workspace into one appropriate to a man carrying out, in addition to his ordinary duties, tasks of solemn importance. Among them was a pair of fine binoculars, which he had placed prominently next to his computer, as well as a few maps of the city, which he had marked in mysterious ways and spread across the surface of the desk.

Every now and then he would glance at these items and feel a little rush of pride and excitement, anticipating the others coming to ask him about this or that one—though he understood that his bearing intimidated them into reticence.

At the fancy restaurant, too, he had reached a new level of confidence. He would bring his valise full of threat items and unpack them at the table—the baseball card and rag, and the preferred snapshots, and on one occasion even the initial threat itself—spreading them into a display and leaning over them in contemplation as he was served course after course by the unflappable waitstaff. He was secretly on fire with the transgressive glee of this exhibitionism. The thought of the others noticing these items was intoxicating, and from time to time he would glance across the room at the coat-check woman, almost breathless with the thought that she was seeing him like *this*, amid the trappings of his predicament! And though he never actually saw her looking at him, he only took that as evidence of her meticulous care to avoid being caught.

He had clipped from a magazine an ad that prominently featured the number thirty-four, thinking that he could show it to her as a joke at some point. He kept the clip in his threat valise but so far had not dared to lay it out on the table with the other items. He would bring it up in time—on a future walk, perhaps. They had not gone on any more walks yet—he had not caught her at the end of her shift—but he thought, with a kind of pleasing self-denial, that now was not really the time for walks anyway, not when he was absorbed with the threat; one day, perhaps soon, he would be free of the threat and then would take her on walk after walk, as many as she desired. And who knows what he would learn of her then—of her apartment, of Viola . . . of acting classes, if she took them . . .

In all aspects of his life, his shield of sophistication was now impregnable, and it protected him from the indignities that had once plagued him. The downstairs neighbor still complained about his walking, but Levin now understood this complaining to be part of the random noise of life—even a billionaire must contend with the sound of a construction worker's jackhammer during his walk—and he actually took pleasure in responding to these complaints, calling out, in a voice drenched in irony, "Sorry!"

If only the complainer could see the way his eyebrows were arched with derision!

He had resumed his visits with Mrs. Cohen, the elderly widow upstairs, once again entering and sitting with her instead of merely dropping at the door the groceries he picked up for her. He took a new delight in these visits. In her presence he felt himself aglow with the majesty of the threat, which she, with her elderly wisdom, must sense. Certainly he never mentioned it; he sipped his tea with stately restraint, then resumed his quiet and upright sitting position while she barraged him with her widowly anecdotes and her grandmotherly compliments—compliments which no longer cowed him, but which he met instead with a wise but appreciative smile. He felt enormously gratified that the threat had ratified all the fulsome praise of hers that had built up over the years, like an unpaid debt—praise that he had suspected was mere grandmotherly fluff but that now he saw as the product of her long experience, a kind of preternatural glimpse of his destiny.

He felt a special joy in that overheated living room—a richer satisfaction than when the purpose of his visits had merely been to relieve her loneliness. Now there was something more; he felt he was extending a kind of indulgence to her by acting as though they were peers—though he felt a genuine kinship with her, too, as though her great agedness had elevated her, at the end of her life, nearer to his plane. Or perhaps this feeling of kinship came from the fact that they shared, each in a different way, a nearness to death. Indeed he had the sense that, without exchanging a word on the topic, they were contemplating that great mystery together, a task that he felt the threat had brought him along with so much else—though in truth he did not have time to get to the bottom of the mysteries of death right now.

And he was happier than ever to accede to her favor-asking, hers and the exerciser's; when Mrs. Cohen specified a fiber supplement for him to pick up, he noted the details with a light heart, full of philanthropic delight, and when the exerciser came to retrieve Mildred, he stood expectantly as though glad and willing to grant the next favor—but she asked for nothing, perhaps sensing that in his new state it was untoward to ask him for things, a misapprehension he tried to allay with extra graciousness.

Most remarkable of all his transformations, he now found himself, steeled with confidence, again and again putting into actual practice the notions that before, repressed by his overdeveloped rectitude, would have shriveled and withered within him, unfulfilled. He would even commit small sins from time to time with glee, as though pricking the callus that had finally formed over his conscience. He stole pens from the supply room; he remained silent when he saw a man on the street walking just ahead of him drop a scrap of paper that might be important.

In short, no longer hemmed in by the rigid rectitude that had suffocated him for so long, he was now a person who breathed the full freedom of life.

He was not without fear of being killed. The fear would still, at times, bubble up suddenly—the image of a knife plunging into his body would come before him with a new vividness, and he would stop what he was doing and clutch his chest as the corrosive poison boiled inside it and his legs underwent their manglings. Or, walking on the street, he would see someone who for a moment he imagined to be coming at him, and he would run in the opposite direction, charged with panic. But he was becoming so used to these things that they were no more an annoyance than bowel movements.

All the while, the threat itself was stationary. There were no escalations: no new notes or threat items, no calls from the threatener, not a peep—which, to the trained eye, was of course no comfort. On the contrary, the silence was menacing—a disquieting and deceptive calm that presaged something shocking on the way. Levin knew that in his lair the threatener was plotting his next move, that it was only a matter of time before his nemesis unleashed the devilish aggression over which he was now diligently at work.

Levin himself would continually think of new ideas for the threat, new inspirations, which he would jot in his notebook. There was one that he was especially pleased with: an odyssey. Inspired by a scene in a movie that he had remembered during his threat contemplations, he imagined the threatener taking him on a long odyssey—a mysterious journey whose destinations would be revealed over the course of the journey itself through hints spoken over the phone by the threatener, who would also direct Levin to perform mysterious tasks, all of course under the ever-renewing threat of death, as though as part of a high-stakes and terrifying treasure hunt . . .

Levin spent long hours envisioning this odyssey with an expression of wonder on his face.

These threat contemplations, and especially the act of writing them down, gave him a terrific sense of productivity. He felt that by envisioning every possible escalation that the threat might undertake, he was doing the hard work of girding himself against those possibilities—a kind of anticipatory defense. But there was something more: he felt, locked in battle with the threatener, an ever-tightening bond with that mysterious enemy—a bond that those who haven't been under the threat of death could never hope to understand and whose logic seemed to equate his own efforts with those of the threatener, to guarantee that in the hours when Levin sweated over the threat, his nemesis was just as hard at work.

But there was no way to convey all this to the rubes who craved threat updates, Levin knew—no way to illustrate, in terms they could grasp with their dull and undiscerning senses, the spectacular menace that this preparatory dormancy of the threat represented.

Levin fretted over this. He felt a kind of responsibility to keep the rubes entertained during this long wait. Leonard in particular was a concern. With his eager eyes and ready tongue, Leonard practically begged to hear of the new adventures and tribulations that the threat had occasioned, and was not going to be assuaged by tales of quiet suspense.

How could Levin convey to them terror that was far more subtle? How could he convey—there was no other way to say it—his faith in the threatener? How could he convey the intimacy of the bond—so strange it would seem to them!—that had developed between the threatener and himself? He wanted to take them aside, to give them comforting hand grasps, and say: "Patience!"

Instead, he hinted darkly that a terrible new escalation was coming.

He would pull Leonard aside in the snack room at odd moments, and with wild eyes say: "I have a feeling we'll have plenty to discuss soon enough."

Then, satisfied with his dark hinting, he wanted to repeat it to everyone in the office in their turn, and would go around inserting similar phrases into conversations with each of them.

It was on Monday again—seven days after he received the first threat, and four days before Adderley's retirement party—that the next package from the threatener arrived.

It was wrapped in brown paper, shaped irregularly as though not boxed but simply wadded up around its contents, and about the size of a newborn. He took it in his hands, gave it a couple of sensible lifts as though to test its weight, then placed it on his desk.

He sat before the unopened package for a long time. "At last!" he thought to himself, over and over, relishing the words. The package seemed to him a concrete achievement, something that he had created out of his efforts—efforts that encompassed not only his long and difficult thinking about the threat but even his staving off of Leonard's enthusiasm until he could present this new escalation. That, too, had been threat work.

He considered taking the package still unopened to the restaurant, placing it on the table as he dined, eyeing it with restraint, drawing out as much as possible the strange pleasure of delayed gratification—but his eagerness was too great, and he finally opened it.

Inside was what Levin for a very brief moment took to be a homemade bomb. But almost immediately he realized that it was in fact a kind of hastily thrown-together doll. It consisted of a paper-towel roll placed inside a sock, representing the torso, with four pipe-cleaners taped on to represent the limbs, and a tennis-ball head with a photo of Levin's face glued onto the front.

Attached to the back of the "torso" was a printed-out picture of a knife, beneath which a stream of blood, trickling down the sock shirt, had been crudely drawn with a marker.

Levin groaned. It was horrible! How could the threatener have been spending these days—days during which Levin had held up his end of their diabolical bargain with conscientious persistence, days during which he had sweated over the threat, had not allowed it to leave his mind for a second—on this awful, shoddy thing?

Levin thought, with alarm and bitterness, of all the dark hintings he had made around the office of the coming escalation—hintings which now, unfulfilled, would taint the credibility of his hinting forever. He could fix the doll, certainly—a million improvements called out immediately, even to someone with no doll-manufacturing experience—but it was going to take so much time that Levin was overcome with resentment at the very idea of it. Was he now to become a doll repairer?

It was so shoddily put together that it would likely fall apart from mere handling. He squeezed it slightly, then shook it gently, expecting it to come apart at once; when it held together, he shook it a bit more, increasing the shaking by degrees until he suddenly in an unforeseen spasm bopped it hard against the desk. The head separated from the body and rolled away.

It was just as he had expected.

He took a deep breath, determined to collect himself. As a man under the threat of death, he could not be so perturbed by setbacks.

He fingered the tacky doll's remains as though his touch could somehow improve it. He knew that he had a duty to acknowledge the threatener's well-meaningness, to credit the fact that the doll in all probability had taken a good deal of effort, that dolls were in all likelihood not the threatener's medium of choice, that it was even possible that he had been pushed, by Levin's suggestions, into an area where he was not fully comfortable.

But he was tired of this constant catering to the threatener's needs.

He did not bother packing the doll into his threat valise the next day, and left for work with a nagging sense almost of guilt, as though by leaving behind a piece of the threat—for it *was* a piece of the threat, that was not for him to decide—he was committing a sin.

He arrived in a sour mood.

The first thing he had to contend with was Leonard's enthusiasm. He approached Levin practically first thing in the morning, and then said—after only brief small talk during which Levin barely mentioned the threat—"Oh yes, the threat! Any updates there?"

Levin tried with all his might not to be overcome by the

poignancy of Leonard's obsession with the threat. How well the poor man meant—how good, in his own pathetic way, he was!

And yet to speak to him of the doll, that shoddy, unworthy thing . . . Levin saw that he would now be forced either to lie or to break Leonard's heart.

A surge of bitterness toward the threatener came over him, but he suppressed it, determined to take pleasure in Leonard's child-like enthusiasm and indulge it to whatever extent he could.

"No updates," Levin said, with a sad shrug.

"Could I see the last note again?"

Levin, genuinely touched, took out his threat valise. "Of course," he said, thinking of weeping. He was not close to actually weeping, but the idea of weeping entered unmistakably into his tone.

Leonard hunched over the note in enthusiasm, and Levin looked on, wistful and pleased.

"Ah . . . yes, yes . . ." Leonard said, his eyes lighting up. "I've been thinking about this."

Levin placed his hand on his chin and put on a kind of pride-ful pout.

"I thought so!" Leonard said suddenly.

And he adjusted his body so that Levin could see he was point-ing to precisely the point where Levin had altered the note.

"See how the ink changes here? It's ever so slight, almost im-perceptible . . ."

Levin grabbed the note back with so much force that Leonard jumped.

"You don't know the first thing about the threat!" Levin yelled.

Then, turning vaguely toward the rest of the office, he cried out: "None of you do!"

Leonard, shocked, scurried away.

Levin sat down. He was himself as stunned as Leonard. It had been the briefest of outbursts, and, looking around, he could see that no one was reacting to it; they were all going on with their non-outburst-related work motions as though they hadn't heard it at all. But Levin was nevertheless overcome by an uncomfortable mixture of anger and shame. Thinking that he should resume a pose of dignified unconcern as quickly as possible—for it was not unlikely that the rubes, even if they were dutifully pretending not to have noticed the outburst, would soon be turning to look his way out of the primal curiosity it had aroused in them—he found himself unable to attain the right posture. He tried posture after posture, but none was able to erase his stunnedness and anger and shame, which seemed implacably lodged in his limbs.

He was glad when the time came for his back exercises, since he could take the opportunity to think things through more soberly, and to reattain his positions of dignity, in the privacy of the lactation room.

Sitting on the gray carpet and bending forward to do his first exercise, he felt his rationality returning to him. He had to curtail these emotional reactions. Distractions were inevitable, be they disappointing dolls or Leonard's uncouthness—these, and far worse, were bound to keep coming from all sides. It was his duty to maintain his equanimity in the face of them. His anger at the threatener's and Leonard's lapses had to be replaced immediately with a certain pitiless, businesslike determination—a low flame that must burn evenly, no matter what winds or jostlings came to disrupt it. It was, he realized, the natural resting state of the man of action he had lately become. The man who walks with coat-check women and takes command of phone calls with his own threatener is one who, when he is not engaged in those acts of daring, still exudes a readiness for them—an imperturbable and passionless neutrality that is ready to convert itself into action at every instant.

And, switching his leaning to the other leg, he smiled, pleased with the quickness with which he had regained his balance.

To Leonard, he would apologize—in time, there was no great rush, for businesslike determination was something that addresses its wrongs at its own convenience, without undue regard for pricks of conscience—and with the threatener he would be at once more patient but also firmer and clearer. The threatener had been confused by Levin's hints about how the threat could escalate—something for which Levin was not without his share of responsibility—and this, too, had to be faced up to with businesslike determination. Faced up to and solved. Taking care of a threat requires action, swift and sure. He would simply have to be more explicit in his suggestions.

As if to give Levin a chance to put this new resolution to the test, the threatener called again that afternoon. Levin, determined to follow the course he had set himself, picked up the call with only the briefest of intense panics.

"How'd you like the doll?" the threatener said.

Levin—after quickly suppressing a surge of disappointment at the realization that the threatener's voice had not gained any additional gravelliness in the time since the first call—took a moment to summon the spirit of his businesslike determination. "I think you've done better things," he said, then cringed at his own bluntness.

"You didn't like it?"

"Look," Levin said, leaning toward the snacks (he was in the snack room to take the call) in a conspiratorial hunch, "I want to take some responsibility for having possibly put you off track."

"What?"

Levin reminded himself that it was no longer a time for hints and double entendres—it was time to be explicit. Later, once the threat was back on track, they could return to the unforgettable repartee of their dances with death.

"Not all threats need to be focused on items. There are other ways that I think could be effective."

"What do you mean?"

"You could . . . toy with me."

"What sort of toying?"

Levin closed his eyes. "An odyssey," he said.

"An odyssey?"

"You choose a journey for me to go on. A destination, or a number of destinations—and you spring it on me without any notice . . ."

Levin, becoming intoxicated by the idea of a mysterious odyssey, was losing his way, unable to choose which of the myriad threads of the magnificent concept with which to begin.

Marla entered the snack room, and Levin glared at her. "I'm on a call!"

"I just want a banana."

Levin peeled off a banana and handed it to her with searing contempt.

When she left, he calmed himself and proceeded to explain the concept of the threat odyssey with great clarity and thoroughness.

"Does that make sense?"

"Yes."

Levin felt almost sentimental at their reconciliation. He looked for something with which to make a gesture of tenderness in order to mark the moment, and seeing only apples—and the bananas, which had been poisoned by their association with Marla's thoughtlessness—he touched the side of one of the apples with two of his fingers, as though smoothing back its hair.

At home that night, Levin took the doll out of its hiding place and regarded it with tenderness. He stroked it a couple of times, and, with something close to love in his eyes, taped the tennis-ball head back on.

He placed the doll on his desk and looked at it from many

different angles, imbuing it through his glances with a menace of its own—the menace of the unexpected, of the not quite right. Before long he was blanching with quite real terror at the thought of it.

He smiled, pleased that he had been able to conjure this terror so effectively. Then he packed it up carefully in his valise with the other threat items.

So the doll, too, in spite of its flaws, took its place in Levin's threat pantheon.

9

THE NEXT DAY, LEVIN APOLOGIZED TO LEONARD WITH extraordinary graciousness. He had spent a fair bit of time rehearsing this apology before leaving for work, and he brought it off with mastery. He placed his hands on Leonard's elbows, looked into his eyes, and delivered an eloquent monologue that, while explaining (by hints) his behavior, did not pretend to excuse it.

"Though the pressures of living under a death threat are immense, immense"—and he closed his eyes to relish this bit of repetition, which, though it had been accidental, he felt was actually a nice bit of rhetoric—"that was no excuse for my behavior."

"Oh, that's fine," Leonard said. "I was thinking that—"

Levin held up his hand peremptorily to stop Leonard from speaking, for he could see, in the distance, Meldon and Flemingson talking quietly together with an air of discussing something important. He wished sincerely to indulge Leonard's blathering, but had become too distracted by the strange sight of this Meldon-Flemingson colloquy, which, in truth, disconcerted him—though only mildly. Meldon and Flemingson could chitchat away—what threat could that pose *him?* In fact, it was cute to see Flemingson trying to put on a dignified bearing as he talked quietly with Meldon—Levin could now see the falseness in it, and could greet that falseness with a smile of mirth.

No, it was nothing to be alarmed by at all—but neither was now the time for complacency. He should, out of an abundance of caution, join them—not with any haste, there was certainly no rush, but wander over in due time as though he had nothing better to do.

There was no sense in waiting, really. The apology had been brought off quite well and was finished, and—seeing Meldon place his hands on the sides of his nose, as though to conceal an expression of shock or perhaps to form a tunnel through which to whisper a secret—Levin moved away from Leonard with something close to a jump and almost ran over to where Meldon and Flemingson were standing.

Without hesitation, Meldon turned to Levin, disassembling his hand tunnel as though it had been nothing at all. "I was just telling Flemingson here that I've been placed in quite the box," Meldon said. "The Chairman of the Board is coming to town tomorrow. It was scheduled for next week, and I was going to have dinner with him and show him a good time. But he's just had to move it up, and I have a family commitment. He's placed me in quite the box, as you can see."

Something important was in the air now. The situation was crucial and required all of Levin's attention. Though it was not explicitly connected with the death threat, still he had the undeniable sense that this visit from the Chairman shared some deep, inarticulable affinity with it.

"The hinges on this one won't budge," Meldon was saying.

All this box talk was making Levin nervous. Nevertheless, he stood tall and unperturbed. The catastrophe of the doll had given rise to a new resolve—as though if he were stronger and more unflinching, he would prevent a bad doll from ever being sent to him again.

"What I've decided to do," Meldon said, "is—"

"I'll go!" Levin shouted.

"I'm sorry?" Meldon said.

"I'll take the Chairman to the dinner," Levin repeated.

They were all stunned—including Levin. Levin's words seemed to have unleashed an explosion. Meldon was blinking his way through some inchoate thoughts; Flemingson, unaccustomed to being stunned, struggled to find a stunned expression. He was certainly far from whistling now. His tall hair stood as if waiting to see how he would react.

"Is that all right?" Meldon finally said to Flemingson. "You do have your mugging appointment to take care of." Turning to Levin, he explained, "He has to go down to the police station."

Levin winced, but only briefly: he supposed Flemingson had to be offered some compensatory sympathy after such a bruising defeat.

"I know just where to take the Chairman," Levin said, hoping that Meldon would ask him to elaborate so that he could tell them of his extraordinary new habit of dining among his fabulously elegant peers. But it was just as well that Meldon didn't ask—after Levin's volunteering, the room couldn't take another stunning.

He retreated to his cubicle, experiencing a new variation of the vibrations he had lately felt in the wake of his boldnesses—only this time, perhaps because the vibrations were the result not just of any bold action but specifically of a victory over a rival, the discomfort was even greater. He felt as though he had won a dangerous fight only by engaging in some unspeakable brutality that—though justified—was destined to be remembered forever afterward with a shudder.

He found his discomfort slightly vexing. He had no reason not to be pleased by what he had done. In all likelihood, Meldon had been on the point of assigning him to take the Chairman to dinner anyway—but his intervention was nevertheless warranted. For he was now a man who, under the threat of death, acted—a man who did not wait for situations simply to unfold, but rather arranged them to his own liking.

And was it really any wonder that he should feel such

discomfort—even pain—from the violation of a habit that had been with him so long as to become an essential part of himself? In order to slough off the rectitude that had confined him for so many years, he would have to cut at it with violent chops.

What terrible things we men under the threat of death must inflict on ourselves!

And, holding himself upright and putting on an expression of appropriate graveness, he thought to himself that he must not allow anything other than the elation of victory to course through him. He had overcome huge challenges, both doll and dinner, and had every reason to be pleased with himself.

After only a few minutes, this determination worked. The discomfort occasioned by his brutal victory dissipated and left behind it only the airy, dizzying joy of the impending dinner. Dinner with the Chairman! His good mood was now impregnable. The annoyances of the remainder of the day were once again reduced to a faint and almost pleasant tickling, because he could smother them with the thought, "Dinner with the Chairman... Dinner with the Chairman..."

And when, in the course of the day, he wished to feel once again the intoxication of his boldness—he was beginning almost not to believe that he had volunteered for the dinner—he walked around the office, among the cubicles, into the snack room, waiting for little conversations to find him in which he could find an excuse to say, "When I go to the dinner ..." or, "It's something I could think about after my dinner ... with the Chairman."

And his skin would flush deeply, his whole body seized by the disorienting force of the words.

All this was child's play, of course. This was no time for thrilling phrases or their accompanying flushes. What he had to do was to prepare for the dinner that, he sensed, would determine the course of his life from now on.

He sat at his desk in a position of great readiness for

preparations. But very quickly he realized there was nothing really to do other than to visualize himself at the dinner (which did provide him with a few more thrilling flushes) and then, when that task also proved less burdensome than expected—because there were not many images left to think of after the main one of him chewing his food next to the Chairman; after a time he was able to add to it shaking the Chairman's hand in greeting (with unbelievable firmness) and patting the Chairman's upper arm with brotherly joviality before they sat down—he was left with nothing but to visualize himself visualizing the dinner.

This he did for many minutes.

He emerged from this effort with a pleasant sense of fatigue, and was even able to face the fact that he had accomplished nothing with surprising unflinchingness. For the truth was that he had, by the strange miraculous inevitability that seemed to surround everything connected with the death threat, been preparing for this dinner for days with as much thoroughness as if he had been told about it ahead of time. What else had he been doing in fashioning his new bearing, in dining at the fabulous restaurant, in making himself known there and even in forging certain connections which could prove useful?

And Levin could perhaps make a remark sometime late in the dinner that subtly indicated the influence he had wielded on the Chairman's behalf . . . a remark that would escape as though by accident—who knows, perhaps he'd have a few drinks; the Chairman, impressed by their collegiality, might even encourage it!—but which would nevertheless hint at the invisible network of influences that had been called upon by Levin throughout the evening in order to enhance the Chairman's visit to Levin's own sphere—a sphere which would seem at once familiar to the Chairman but also enticingly foreign, like some location familiar from childhood as it appears transfigured in a pleasant dream.

When Marla came by to ask if he'd gotten the napkins for

Adderley's retirement party yet, he was able to laugh and say, "Napkins? Why, yes, I'll get them, after my dinner with the Chairman!"—and the fact that she didn't laugh at this almost cosmic joke evoked only pity in him.

"I'm glad you haven't gotten them yet, because we decided on a color scheme."

"A color scheme!" Levin crowed sarcastically. "Why, of course!"

"The napkins should be purple and yellow. Make sure of that."

"Oh, I certainly will," Levin said, with ostentatious sarcasm. He had struck upon the delightful notion of immediately forgetting the colors that Marla had requested, forcing himself to pick the napkins at random and return—in all likelihood—with the wrong ones. Let them see what things occupied his mind—things that made napkin colors seem quite ridiculous!

"Purple and yellow," Marla said as she walked away.

And Levin realized, with bitter resentment, that he would never forget those colors, not for the rest of his life.

He cheered himself by turning his thoughts again to the preparations for the dinner.

The sight of his coat hanging on the hook by his cubicle caught his eye. He had been putting off procuring a new death-threat wardrobe. His preexisting clothes had been sufficing surprisingly well; they seemed to have acquired, by the bearing with which he now wore them, an unexpected elegance. He had even been checking his lesser coats with the coat-check woman with a kind of abandon. But now, the dinner with the Chairman seemed the occasion to take further action.

He went to Meldon's office and knocked on the open door—there was no longer any need to hesitate about this kind of thing—and pushed in when Meldon looked up. Levin meant to make a strong declaration. He said: "I need to go out to do some preparations for the dinner." He was quite satisfied with the remark. But then, seeing that Meldon seemed unsure, he was forced to add: "Would that be all right?"

"Sure," said Meldon, who then looked back down at his work, no doubt out of a wish not to dwell on Levin's increasing power over him.

But where could he find the proper attire? He thought at once of the coat-check woman. She was a person who handled many, many fine garments as a matter of course, and she might well have picked up one or two hints along the way about how to procure them. She would understand at once, with her huge eyes that broadcast understanding, the importance of selecting a wardrobe that befitted his predicament and his standing. But he dismissed this idea quickly: he simply could not ask her such a thing—not out of embarrassment for himself, but because of how it would disconcert *her*, would shake the foundations of her worldview, to suddenly learn that a man such as he didn't even have a reliable tailor! It would easily be the most distressing incident in her life since her last tiff with Viola.

Then he remembered that he had seen, more than once, one of the lawyers in the elevator carrying a garment bag labeled with the name "Antonio's." Levin smiled when he recalled the elegance of that bag, the neatness and delicacy of the compact lettering—though the mere name, Antonio's, with its foreign flavor, was enough to convince him that his problem was solved.

He looked up the shop's location and saw that it was not as easy to get to as he might have liked—but rather than be annoyed, he actually was pleased that the errand would require effort. He was really working, penetrating deeply into what he needed to do—whether it was for the threat or for the dinner with the Chairman he would not have been quite able to articulate, but the sense of productivity was deep and undeniable.

10

T HE TAILORING SHOP WAS EVERYTHING HE COULD have hoped for. It was a dark little basement space, filled with shadows and crowded with swaths of cloth and fine pencils left on tables.

The tailor was a compact, silver-haired man whose impeccably shaped mustache seemed a testament to his tailoring skill. He barely spoke English, and Levin was delighted by his foreignness. Of course it now seemed ridiculous to think that a domestic tailor could have constructed a death-threat outfit. Once again, Levin's instincts had steered him correctly.

The tailor allowed himself only the occasional word, as though aware that he must guard the charm of his accent by disbursing it sparingly. The silence with which he mainly communicated gave Levin a strange sense of understanding. He would have liked to explain how important the outfit was; how crucial it was that a man in his position construct an appearance that exuded that position—and at the same time he knew that to try to explain this in words would inevitably be inadequate, that words would somehow degrade these lofty notions. But in the tailor's smiling concentration, and the meticulous precision with which he moved the tape over Levin's body and jotted down the measurements in crisp pencil markings, Levin sensed an expression of understanding of his predicament deeper and more comprehensive than any that could have been communicated with mere words. Here was a man who no doubt, even in his relatively short time in the country, had tailored many important men, and through the special intimacy of that bond had gained—if not an understanding of the ins and outs of their higher existence in minute detail—enough of an understanding to know that what was due to them was awed respect.

And, as though to ratify Levin's wisdom in coming here, the tailor brought out a terrific navy suit that, off the shelf, fit Levin perfectly. He bought it on the spot.

The bill caused Levin to blanch in fright. But he calmed himself with the thought that the Chairman would take one look at the fabulous suit and know the score: that Meldon had done right to send as his emissary someone who took a death threat in stride.

He left the shop wearing his new suit, brimming with satisfaction. The very air, mild and full of the promise of spring, was dense with anticipation. In fewer than twenty-four hours he would walk through these streets—well, not exactly these streets; but ones fairly nearby and certainly very similar—with the Chairman!

He wanted to skip—to skip through the streets! But, knowing full well that skipping was undignified—an indulgence men on the higher plane do not permit themselves even in the most exuberant circumstances—he placed the skips into his eyes, which he imagined to be sparkling with childlike joy as he began to walk home with responsibly conservative steps.

He would skip later, at home, even if only briefly—the downstairs complainer be damned.

Still, in spite of his satisfaction, he felt a nagging sense of incompleteness, as though there must be something else he could do to ensure a smooth dinner. It was likely no more than yet another curse of the great man's lot—the ineradicable sense that a duty of such huge magnitude and import can never really be completed—for, from a practical point of view, everything had been done. He had prepared the whole itinerary, deciding on the way to the tailoring shop that he would take the Chairman to a museum first, give him a taste of the city's cultural offerings that they as higher men savored, before taking him to dinner at the fancy restaurant . . . the restaurant that would stun the Chairman with its elegance . . .

And he realized that he had an overpowering urge to go to the restaurant right now and, as a last precaution, speak to the coat-check woman, to let her know how important the dinner was—important even by his own lofty standards—and to ask her, as a favor to him, to make sure everything was looked after especially well.

It couldn't hurt to make a cursory visit. It would be going too far to make special arrangements with the manager; to do that would be, in a sense, cheating—rigging the game in a way that was unseemly. Even to speak to the maître d', Levin felt, would be taking too great a step in this official direction. But the coat-check woman was perfectly positioned. She was not so high in the organization that his asking would be over the top, but she was certainly not without influence; and after all, this was a woman with whom he had gone on a walk, a woman whose roommate's name he knew—a woman, that is to say, with whom he did not have to mince words. Though given the depth of this intimacy, he would not even have to say anything explicit: he could maintain a perfect cover of unconcern.

Delighted, he stopped at his apartment to drop off the clothes he had been wearing before he had changed into the suit. He even left his coat there—the evening was mild enough that he didn't need it—and the thought that he would now approach the coat-check woman while coatless came to him with a kind of maniacal, intoxicating thrill. He was ready for that now. Charged with nervous excitement, he rushed to the restaurant with hurried steps at first, then at a full jog, thinking that he had been so punctilious in cultivating his death-threat gait that he was entitled to a brief jog.

She was standing at her usual post, her sweet face raised in greeting, her receding chin (he almost had to castigate himself for having thought of it that way) now seeming to indicate a certain approachability, as though a flaw (if it could be called a flaw!) were necessary to dilute what would otherwise be a forbidding perfection, and her striking eyes indicating a state of readiness— for coats, of course, but it was a readiness that extended to other things too, to anything he might throw at her: she would take it up with the same beguiling gracefulness with which she handled all the city's finest outer garments. Her hair was tucked neatly behind her ears; probably she had brushed it back with two fingers not long before.

He walked over to the coat-check window and tapped on its marble counter with his fingers. Such liberties were now old hat for him, and, almost in an attempt to reawaken the amazement he had once felt at his own boldness, he continued his tapping and even moved his hands left and right across the counter as though playing the piano.

She smiled to indicate that his tapping was welcome. Her brazen lack of any reference to his not having a coat—either verbally or in gesture—was telling. Though not, of course, surprising. He leaned slightly forward, and said, with a jocular smile, "I've been thinking *thirty-four* times of coming here."

She chuckled a bit, probably slightly exceeding the strict decorum in doing so.

But in spite of how well it was going, Levin realized that he was stuck. He had felt, jogging over, that he possessed within the reaches of his mind the words and gestures that would convey, with perfect subtlety and eloquence, his request. Now he realized with a rush of anxiety that in fact he had in mind nothing more than the "thirty-four" joke that he had already delivered.

"Thirty-four times," he said again, somewhat wistfully, as though already imagining the days when they would remember these remarks with nostalgia. But in reality he was buying time. He could banter with her as long as he liked, but what good would that really do him? He had to come to the heart of the matter eventually.

"Listen," he said suddenly, "I'm not here to check a coat."

"Oh," she said with some surprise. Evidently she had only now noticed his coatlessness.

Levin looked at her. In her striking eyes there was a new note, unfamiliar to him in spite of all his long contemplation of her expressions. Her eyes were wide—but, inexplicably, rather than exude their characteristic sweetness, the wideness seemed to conceal it. There was almost a note in this new expression—Levin was dismayed to discern it, but he would not censor any avenue of investigation into her face simply because it was uncomfortable, as though out of some medieval propriety that impedes the march of knowledge—of fear.

Somewhat disconcerted, Levin momentarily lost his footing and began to stammer. The coat-check woman, perhaps reacting to Levin's stammer, blushed, and Levin, seeing the blush, was disturbed further, which increased his stammering.

He saw at once that he was trapped in a dangerous, unbreakable cycle of blushing and stammering. Therefore, when his phone rang, he pulled it out with some relief, and answered without looking.

It was the wheezy, distant voice of the threatener that spoke: "It's time for your odyssey."

Never had the threatener's voice been more of a comfort to him, since he could now delight in putting on motions of busyness to the coat-check woman—who, incredibly and thrillingly, was inches away from the sound of the voice of the threatener himself!

Of course he also, at the sound of the threatener's voice, felt himself taken by his usual bout of extraordinary panic.

From amid the whirl that everything had become, he thrust up his hand to indicate: "Just a moment, I've an important call," and spun around to leave—too quickly, for he wished he had taken the time to savor the gesture, to imprint the image of the coat-check woman's reaction on his mind!

"All right," Levin said, walking outside.

He had said it with a swaggering smirk, which he displayed widely for all to see. He was ready to engage in another *pas de deux* with his opponent, ready to use every ounce of his own smarts and wiles to defeat him—but at the same time he had reached a level of maturity to be able to slow down and admonish himself to avoid repeating the mistake he had just made with his gesture of busyness and to savor this experience, to etch it on his memory in gilded script, for it would perhaps be his only death-threat odyssey, and he might one day look back on it with tender longing.

"You certainly thought of one fairly quickly," Levin went on, realizing that the threatener had lapsed into one of his habitual silences.

"I was planning this before you mentioned it."

Levin frowned at this obvious lie, but resolved not to let it ruin things.

"Head to the cemetery," the threatener said.

Now Levin winced. Did the threatener not understand the first thing about odysseys? He shouldn't immediately announce the destination—he should lead Levin there by hints and toyings! Thinking of all the ways there were to toy with someone on the phone, to hint by degrees, Levin was almost overcome with disappointment.

"Did you want to hint by degrees?" Levin said.

"Excuse me?"

Levin admonished himself to be patient. Perhaps what would transpire at the cemetery would surprise him.

But immediately he realized that he had to ask the threatener another question. "How do you want me to get there?"

"However you want," the threatener said, and gave him the address.

Levin was annoyed. It was a decision that the threatener ought to have made himself.

"This is under the threat of death, right?" Levin asked.

"Yes."

Somewhat heartened, Levin hailed a taxi.

This turned out to be a miscalculation. The taxi ride was excruciating. The driver, a wide man with a horizontal face and a predilection for boisterous jazz, kept asking small-talk questions at intervals. Levin's monosyllabism, expertly deployed, successfully put the driver off—but only temporarily, and after six or seven minutes the moratorium would expire and he would try again. Even the phone pressed against Levin's ear, which he displayed with a few ostentatious head-turns, had no effect on the driver's attempts.

"Are you doing anything for Easter?"

"No," Levin said, trying to inject enough bitter sharpness into the word to lengthen the next small-talk moratorium—even another minute would do him good.

All the while, the threatener said nothing. Only his labored breathing came through, and, occasionally, the wet clacking. Levin scowled. He wished with all his might that they could return to the *pas de deux* of their initial call. But Levin couldn't think of how to launch into a *pas de deux*, which after all requires the active contributions of both parties by definition. And anyway it certainly was not possible to have a death-threat *pas de deux* in the presence of boisterous jazz.

When they finally reached the cemetery, Levin allowed more of his impatience to enter his voice. "So now what?"

The cemetery, which the threatener had probably expected to be the most mysterious and menacing place on earth, was, of course, totally bereft of mystery and menace. Anyone with any aesthetic sense could have guessed it! It was unkempt, but not a creepy unkemptness. It was the banal unkemptness of a disordered closet. The dull, overgrown grass put one in mind of a Little League field just out of season. The headstones—modern, with machine-hewn angles and cheap shining surfaces—lacked even a hint of hauntedness. Of course, at this point it could not be safely assumed that the threatener had even staked out the cemetery ahead of time. Levin was unsure which was more distasteful: that possibility, or that he had taken a thorough look at this drab affair and thought, "Perfect for an odyssey."

And if he were to be killed . . . here? His corpse found in this cemetery like some tacky Halloween decoration?

He could not help but envision the hypothetical corpses of his rightful peers—of the lawyers, of Meldon, even (dare he think it?) of the Chairman—corpses that, should these men ever be murdered, would no doubt turn up in far more respectable circumstances.

The threatener's continued silence was beginning to annoy him greatly. Levin grumbled, "Hello! Hello!"

"Yes," the threatener said finally.

"Well, what is it then? What am I supposed to do?"

"Read some of the gravestones."

Levin looked around. "Aloud, or . . . ?"

"Yes, aloud."

Levin read off a few of the names. Then, when this was met with more silence, he asked, "Should I keep reading?" Obviously the threatener hadn't thought the odyssey through at all. He was improvising—badly. He was not made to improvise. He was a threatener who needed to plan things in advance very carefully.

Levin's impatience was becoming almost unbearable.

"Lie down on the grave," the threatener said finally.

Levin wanted to roll his eyes. "Look, maybe if we hang back a minute, we can think—"

"Lie down on the grave."

"On which grave?"

"The last one you said. Richard . . ."

"Robert Perkins?"

"Yes. Robert Perkins."

"Listen, I appreciate your efforts here . . ."

"Lie down on it!"

Levin eyed the grave with more disdain than dread. The dirt around the gravestone was wet and mossy. It had not been made for lying in, whether as part of a coerced odyssey or for any other reason. It would ruin his death-threat clothes, his fine new suit— Levin could tell that at a single glance, without any great expertise in clothes-soiling.

"You're watching me?" Levin asked.

"Yes."

"You're watching me right now, and you'll kill me if I don't do it?"

"Yes."

Levin looked left and right. There was no one. True, graves and trees made good hiding places. Even in the full light of day, a graveyard was certainly an ideal place for concealed spying, let alone now, with night falling fast.

Nevertheless, he was suddenly possessed by a firm and un-shakeable certainty: *the threatener is not here and cannot see you.*

The certainty was so great—though it would have been difficult to say exactly what its basis was—that he barely felt the need to test it. He did, half-heartedly, raise his left arm and wave it around, which elicited no comment from the threatener. Then, with barely more energy, he made a more unorthodox motion, sweeping his left arm in a figure-eight and thrusting out his left foot in a few kicks.

The threatener said nothing.

"Now, let's be reasonable," Levin told the threatener calmly, returning to a mode of hyper-rational, strategic coaxing, as though his strange motions, having gone unseen, could be erased from history. "You are a reasonable threatener, and I respect that about you. So let me make a reasonable request, which I think you will reasonably grant. I don't have on the outfit for lying on graves."

"I don't care."

"You didn't tell me to wear grave-lying clothes, which I would gladly have done."

"Lie down on the grave."

"What about a different degradation? There are plenty I could do in my suit."

"Lie on the grave."

"I could steal something. I could come up with five or six more suggestions, and you can reject them all and I'll come up with more," Levin said, having intended to list specific things before realizing he could only think of one.

"No," the threatener said.

Levin appreciated, grudgingly, the threatener's stubbornness. His impatience with the threatener was unfair in some measure. Just because his threatener was perhaps on uneasy ground with improvising an odyssey, that did not make him someone to toy with. Nor was there anything that Levin could rightly object to in the idea of being humiliated *per se*. As part of a well-constructed threat, humiliation was not only acceptable but even inevitable— but it ought to be done in a sophisticated way that was appropriate to his station. To soil his fine suit on a grave that had not even been selected with any purpose—there was no escaping the utter vulgarity of it. It was the shoddy doll of odyssey tasks. That is what he wished to convey to the threatener, whose ears seemed hopelessly closed to this kind of persuasion.

"What about another grave?" Levin asked.

"LIE DOWN ON—" the threatener began to yell with real menace, but then broke into an unending hacking cough.

Levin looked around again. Each hacking cough seemed to chip away at the dwindling reserve of his patience and good will for the threatener, and to reveal more and more a well of contempt.

The coughing went on and on.

And he realized what he must do. He must remember that he was now, after all, a man who takes situations into his own hands—a man no longer hemmed in by the rectitude that had once crippled him. As a man of action—as a man with dinners with the Chairman on his mind—he need not stand for every single inconvenience. *Could* not stand for them.

He lifted his chin to a dignified angle, and, though he knew the threatener was nowhere around, still flaunted the upraised chin in all directions, if only to launch himself into the new tone of voice which he now intended to adopt.

"Certainly," Levin said into the phone. And, great expert though he had become at placing ironic layers into his cadences, he allowed this one to be slathered with a single rather simple and unsubtle note: defiance. "Certainly I will."

"Okay," said the threatener.

"I'll do it right after I hang up."

And Levin ended the call.

He stared at the chosen grave, which read: "Robert Perkins: Friend to Birds." In that stony monument, with its strange epitaph, it seemed that his fate was spelled out, if only he could discern the code.

Levin had already taken one rash action, by hanging up on

the threatener. Now it remained to complete the apotheosis of his transformation, to bring the flowering of his newfound defiance to full bloom. He would now turn from the grave, from this whole charade, with his head upturned, his expression full of condescending loathing, his bearing full of majesty. Yes, far from mere dignity, far from a mere death-threat bearing, Levin was now ablaze with majesty! Here is what he thought of a grave on which he was meant to lie for some invisible threatener who certainly was not there: he would spit on it! Yes, he would spit upon the grave—with apologies to Robert Perkins; Robert, it is not you that I spit upon, but the utter absurdity of a man of my position being turned into the plaything of a threatener who lacks basic competence!

He was on the point of doing it. He even began to prepare the spit motion—but at the last second he arrested the spit muscles, swallowed the prepared saliva, and, with a quiet swiftness as though to convince himself that the motion was automatic, he ran to the grave, crouched down, and—resolving to take great care to hold his body suspended above the ground by an inch or two, so that to any observer it would seem that he was (perfunctorily enough!) fulfilling his duty, but without soiling his precious new suit—lowered himself toward the grave in a swift and almost elegant motion, intending to bring himself back up, unsoiled, at once.

But at the crucial moment, his back erupted in a spasm of pain. He lost control of his body and he ended up edging a large portion of his left arm and side into the mound of shining mossy dirt.

He stood back up, stunned, taking stock of the sullying. The new suit was smudged with a huge amount of the dirt. It was ruined.

He was furious. He let out an otherworldly wail; and then, having liked the wail, and having looked around to confirm that no one had heard it, he let out another—but the second lacked all the unique abandon of the first.

He looked around desperately for other ways he could disperse his anger, then wandered for a few frantic minutes among the graves, fevered images of kickings and wild runnings going through his mind.

But in the end, he left without having done anything more than a few additional half-hearted wails.

At home, he began the arduous business of collecting himself. He stood before the ruined suit, hanging across his closet door, as though it might speak the answers he needed. The huge stain—to which his glance returned again and again, as though hoping each time to discover that all the previous lookings had deceived him—was, in the context of a suit that had ratified his position on the higher plane, almost shockingly profane. It was a mockery of his act of defiance, a desecration so extreme as to be almost comical.

His act of defiance . . .

But hadn't he, in fact, performed the act of defiance?

Yes. Just because he had slipped while performing it did not nullify its underpinning defyingness.

And all at once he almost had to laugh. It had been his own mistake, after all—not the threatener's!—to slip into the dirt. Mistakes were mistakes—even men such as he were not immune to them—and they did not simply negate everything when they occurred! A slip here and there could not be permitted to assume any more significance, in the face of the fabulous act of defiance he had performed, than that of a joking remark inserted as an aside into a profound and moving parable.

Not wanting to let this moment of genuine mirth pass too quickly, he forced himself to laugh briefly.

But then, without overindulging this jovial respite, he quickly brushed his teeth and went right to bed.

For, in the morning, the day would dawn when he would take the Chairman to dinner. The sullying of a suit, from threat activity, was not going to get in the way of such a thing as that.

The wailer kept him up a fair bit longer than he would have liked, but even this did not greatly perturb him.

11

THE CHAIRMAN WAS TO ARRIVE AT FIVE O'CLOCK, AND by three Levin was glued to his chair, reluctant to leave his desk even for a minute lest the Chairman arrive while he was gone. The two times he had to go to the bathroom, he went with such haste that he didn't fully void his bladder before rushing back to his cubicle.

He was prepared. He had breakfasted well, in spite of a nervous lack of hunger, and practiced his gait—but only briefly—before walking to work, filled with a singular focus. He had, it was true, picked up the fiber supplements for Mrs. Cohen—when he passed the health store where he knew they sold them, the temptation to stop in had been irresistible—but he had purchased the pills quickly and stowed them in his pocket hastily, returning his thoughts once again to the rarefied task ahead of him, feeling that matters such as fiber supplements ought not to be contemplated for too great a duration on a day such as this, a day fraught with importance.

And now in the afternoon he sat, waiting, in calm confidence.

For he had decided, after much complicated consideration, that the main topic of conversation between himself and the Chairman—fate had practically decreed it—would be the threat.

Yes: he would bring it up! The Chairman was a man who was made for the threat as a topic—a man who would understand it at a glance, in a way that even Meldon was not truly capable of. Meldon was no rube, of course, and Levin did not wish to imply that he was—but still, it was time for Levin to begin mixing on even higher planes now, with all due respect to his boss, for whom he would never lose a certain nostalgic respect no matter how high he himself rose.

Levin was still not certain exactly how he would broach the subject of the threat with the Chairman. He was undecided between a gradual approach, starting with a preamble, or—and this possibility thrilled him to such a degree that it caused his skin to erupt into a mild burning sensation when he thought of it—springing it upon him without warning... suddenly slip into the conversation some remark such as, "I've been threatened..."

The Chairman would not blink at such shocks! His eyes might widen for a split second—for even among those used to life-and-death concerns, Levin's threat was still on the more serious side of things—but then he would recall the person with whom he was dealing, and perhaps he would reveal that he even suspected something like this might be the case—perhaps not in so many words, perhaps only with a glance, and perhaps not specifically a threat. But the idea of it would surprise him so little that he might imagine that he had even heard about it before, as though it were a vaguely familiar detail from a dream.

For the Chairman was a man—tall, imposing, monumental, with a face well stocked with dignified furrows—who was made for the higher plane of existence. He was a person whose dignity and bearing were automatic, the product of the sheer force of his physicality. He was born, in other words, already in possession of what others must carefully cultivate. People like Levin had to work hard to build up their death-threat miens and bearings—which did not mean they were any less worthy of them, but it was possible for these types (and they surely formed the vast majority of important men) to miss their calling and never cultivate what was their due. Not so for men such as the Chairman.

And yet now Levin would be able to walk side by side with such a man in a certain harmony. They would walk down the street, and not one person would stare in surprise, not a single on-looker would say, "What an odd pair."

At one point as he waited, Marla came up to him and—in flagrant disregard for the gravity of his waiting—began talking to him without any apology or even greeting.

"I was thinking the napkins should be cat napkins," she said.

"What are you talking about?" He was perfectly aware of what she was referring to, but wished to punish her for her presumption in assuming that he did.

"For the party. They have cat napkins," and she named the supply store where Levin was to go to get them.

He widened his eyes and tried to push his pain through them.

"Fine," he said finally, when she did not react to the pain eyes.

"And yellow and purple, remember."

"*Fine*," Levin said, with unbelievable pique.

He returned to staring toward the office entrance.

Finally the door opened and the Chairman emerged. Levin stood immediately and began to walk toward the entrance, doing his best death-threat walk and putting on the smile that he had practiced so much—though now that the moment so long anticipated had arrived, it came with such disorienting vividness that he was only able to access his preparation intermittently and in part—and then noticed that Meldon and Flemingson were also converging on the entrance area. It was as though they had been conspiring to enter a race with Levin without telling him. Levin smirked. So they fancied themselves participants in a competition with him! Well, all right, let them join him in his greeting—and then slink back to their dull lives as he continued on with the Chairman, doing things they could only dream of.

He noticed that the pain in his back had flared up—perhaps from standing too quickly.

Then Levin realized with a rush of terror that the Chairman was shifting his gaze back and forth between Levin and Flemingson as they approached, with what might conceivably be an expression of perplexity. Was it possible that he did not know which one Levin was? Inconceivable as it was, now was not the time for complacency: when you see in the distance that your home is on fire, you don't start elucidating all the reasons why such a thing is unlikely!

Levin thrust his hand out—even though the Chairman was still about a dozen feet away—and then a moment later, worried that even this premature thrusting might not be sufficient, said in a strong and clear voice: "Levin!"

He added an ironic smile, an amused narrowing of his eyes, and a jovial sideways toss of his head—to hint that his saying his name was a kind of joke between them. He was going to add a chuckle but did not have time.

"Hello," said the Chairman, shaking all three men's hands, as Levin smiled at his own quick thinking. The greeting had not gone as he had planned, but then improvisations had to be relied on sometimes, as the Chairman should well know. In games of life and death, you plan and plan—and then throw it all to the wind at the highest-pressure moment.

Meldon and the Chairman began to speak of the Chairman's travel, and all the while Levin could detect the Chairman throwing him a few conspiratorial glances in acknowledgment of the coming dinner—as though to say, "Soon you and I will be free of this small talk . . . Bear with me."

Eventually, Meldon said, "Unfortunately I'm unable to go to dinner tonight. Levin here will be taking you."

"I see," the Chairman said. "Fine, fine."

Levin blanched—so the Chairman hadn't known! Unless this too was some type of charade—possibly for Flemingson's benefit. Levin remained remarkably calm. He reasoned that the Chairman, if indeed he was hearing the news of Levin's accompanying him for the first time, had taken it with perfect equanimity. It certainly said something about Levin's qualifications as host that the Chairman wouldn't bat an eye when informed of a change like this out of the blue in front of others.

Nevertheless, Levin felt the need to do something to reestablish his own primacy. He struck on it at once: he leaned toward the Chairman and whispered in his ear: "I thought we would go to the museum before dinner." The Chairman nodded, delighting Levin. "Fine, fine," he said—and Levin was thrilled that the others would have to guess, in futility, what those "fines" referred to!

Then the Chairman turned to Flemingson. "Flemingson, right? I heard you went through a bit of a scare recently."

Levin frowned. He knew it was only right for the lesser lights to get their brief chance to be displayed now, before serious matters got under way. Flemingson could have his consolation prize.

And before long, they were off.

On the walk to the museum, the conversation flowed easily, as it should between two important men. Levin needn't have worried about this (as about so much else!), for he was able to hold the Chairman's interest with very little effort by reeling off some of the recent developments in the branch. Once again, as during his walk with the coat-check woman, some guardian seemed to be guiding him to the exact right words again and again. The Chairman engaged with each topic in his laconic way, with a hearty "Fine!"— and even the occasional "Is that so?"—and Levin began to feel almost a sense of discomfort at how easily he could elicit enthusiastic words from the Chairman. With a bit of embarrassment, he imagined himself before some poor sucker who would expend all his strength and barely be able to wrench a half-audible "okay" from a man such as this, while Levin, with hardly any effort, had at his disposal an endlessly renewable repository of *Fine!*s and *Is that so?*s that bristled with energy.

At one point Levin noticed, as the Chairman was adjusting his collar, that there was a large, elongated, brown stain on his right cuff.

Levin was astonished. Could someone such as the Chairman have been so careless?

From then on, Levin noticed that the stain was visible not only during chance adjustments, but—to the eye that was aware of it— at all times. He was taking no pains to conceal it!

Shocked and reeling, Levin tried to make sense of this unbelievable fact. It seemed to Levin that it was not some kind of unintentional lapse on the Chairman's part—such a thing was inconceivable—but a kind of provocativeness, a burlesquing of the lower orders that had a certain outrageous daring to it, as though for the Chairman—a man for whom inhabiting the higher plane was such a longstanding and unremarkable thing that it had actually become boring and occasionally required spicing up by unconventional means—a flagrantly displayed cuff stain was a kind of crazed, outré game in which, to make life interesting, he danced upon the boundaries that mark the edge of the civilized.

It brought a grin to Levin's face, for he had the unmistakable sense that, in putting on this outrageous display, the Chairman was quite deliberately inviting Levin into a greater intimacy. Such louche jokes were made only among close confidants. Levin had to suppress the urge to glance coquettishly at the cuff stain, to tilt down his head and say, "Mr. *Chairman!*"

At the museum, Levin congratulated himself on his excellent

idea in coming here. The works of art afforded the perfect opportunity to showcase the incredible strides he had made in displaying his dignity. How easy it was to lean toward a painting or sculpture with furrowed brows, intense with contemplation, and to shake one's head as though in awe—and how many opportunities there were to repeat this gesture in its hundred variations, painting by painting!

Once, as Levin was looking at a certain painting, he saw, out of the corner of his eye, what appeared to be someone walking toward him rather quickly, and, overcome with fear that the threatener was about to kill him, his heart galloped, and he was flooded with a corrosive anxiety that tempted him to collapse to the floor and scream as loudly as he could. But he did not collapse and scream. Instead, he steeled himself, screwing up his face and tensing with all possible effort against the onrush of fear until it passed. It was like letting a truck run over him. When it abated, realizing that his face had evinced an extreme grimace and that he had let out a minor yelp, Levin adeptly turned these things into a reaction to the painting before him, hinting that it was the power of its art that had transported him to another realm. He turned back to the painting and did a few more sounds, similar to the yelp but tending in the direction of transcendent rapture.

He had pulled it off brilliantly, he thought, and he took one last glance at the painting, which showed a bunch of grapes on a silver platter, as though in gratitude to it.

But for the most part, their march through the galleries was unimpeded. They could work their way through the museum for hours on end if necessary, showing each other their dignified bearings, and Levin had only to be careful that he didn't accidentally bring them to the same room twice.

Nevertheless, Levin would have had to admit that his

attention was not fully on keeping track of which paintings they had seen. He was transfixed by the Chairman, and still unable to dismiss from his mind the unbelievable shock of his provocative cuff stain. To think that beneath that jacket sleeve, that *very* sleeve . . .

He looked around at the tourists and other museumgoers—who had no idea, of course!

Levin had been let in on a kind of secret—the secret of flaws that were shown only to those on the higher plane. You don't speak of them—certainly not to outsiders, but probably not even among the initiated, not openly. So that if someone were to ask what the dinner had been like, you would never mention the cuff stain.

As if he had heard these thoughts and wished to ratify them, at that very moment the Chairman let burst a tremendous honking nose-blow into a wadded tissue. Levin heard this honk with a secret, transgressive flush. He cowered slightly, burying his mouth in his fists, as though overhearing a terrible, lurid confession.

Then he had an idea. He slowly removed a tissue from his own pocket and looked at it with sly daring.

Wasn't he a man on the higher plane—didn't he have every right to engage in outré displays?

He stared at the tissue, overcome with a thrilling fear. Did he dare? It seemed that it would be the perfect way for him to have a first dalliance with this newfound sanctified zone—while at the same time sending a kind of call to the Chairman, a signal of covert understanding and consent.

But as he was about to let fly the honking blow—the prepared phlegm a kind of reservoir of his incredible daring—he panicked and cancelled the blow, crumpling the tissue and moving his gaze around the room in a consciously nonchalant fashion, as though to imply that the reason for his sudden change of mind must be located in something he had noticed.

There would be time enough later on for outré nose-blowings, he reasoned—time enough for all such hidden refinements, time enough to enjoy them after discovering them one by one, after unraveling all the most arcane puzzles in whose solutions lay the way to the higher life's most perfect fulfillment.

He snorted the phlegm quietly, filled with the joy of faith in a tranquil future.

Later, as they walked to the restaurant, Levin felt himself enwrapped as though by a warm blanket that was this faith in the future. He felt assured that he would overcome the threat just as he was now overcoming obstacle after obstacle—that it would soon be nothing but a figment of his past, and he would be left only with the developed self with which he had met its menace.

He opened the restaurant door for the Chairman, grasping with vigor the huge, weighty metal of its handle as though in an expression of the heartiness he was feeling, and gestured with extreme grace for the Chairman to enter before him—but not before stealing a glance at the magnificence inside, so that he could have it fresh in his mind as he watched the Chairman walk in. He had the sense that the restaurant was his own creation that he was now revealing to the Chairman.

"I think you'll like it here," Levin said, relishing the understatement.

"Fine, fine," the Chairman said.

"We'll just check our coats," Levin said, and he couldn't help but blow up his cheeks in a kind of burst of devilish excitement at this idea—he felt as though he were leading the Chairman through the last stage of an elaborate ruse that would end with a surprise party—"And then—"

But Levin didn't finish, for he was distracted by his phone ringing.

He pulled it out and saw that it was an unidentified caller.

Terrified, he answered.

"Yes?"

"It's the threatener."

"Yes, hello."

"It's time for your next odyssey," the threatener said.

Levin was seized by an uncomfortable feeling akin to nausea, except that it was in his entire body.

"It's not a good time," he said, moving away from the Chairman.

"I thought we'd go to the amusement park."

Levin tensed in frustration. "Why do you insist on telling me the destination for the odyssey!"

"Why not?"

"It's not a good time for an odyssey right now."

"*Make* it a good time, my friend."

"Listen," Levin said, trying to be diplomatic, "first, let me say how much I admire what you're doing with the odysseys."

"Cram it," the threatener said.

Levin winced but steeled himself to go on. "Let's be reasonable. We're both men of busy schedules and immense responsibilities. I will gladly be at your disposal for an odyssey at a time of your choosing, and will even be willing to do an additional odyssey to make up for my being indisposed for this one."

"The odyssey starts right now."

"Please!" Levin said, too loudly. And then, as if he could cancel that loudness by saying it a second time, he repeated more quietly: "Please."

"Start walking to the subway and tell me when you're there."

The sight of the Chairman, looking closely at a framed magazine article that was hanging on the wall, and the sight of the coat-check woman, who was handling the coat of another patron with a bit more indolence than usual, steeled something in Levin. He must not allow them to see him accede to these wishes, disrupting the dinner. He must not allow them to see him revert to the earlier version of himself, a man who does not act. He was now a man who, under the threat of death, takes what he needs without apology—who walks with coat-check women and volunteers for important dinners. He was, in fact, a man who had defied his threatener already, at the graveyard, notwithstanding his small slip—and this time there would be no slip. He understood that his botched grave-lying had been a kind of dress rehearsal for this much more important performance.

He would now defy his threatener with the ease of someone declining a cup of coffee that he did not want.

"No," Levin said into the phone, with icy calm.

"What?"

Levin cleared his throat, wishing to voice his defiance with the utmost clarity. "No."

"Then I'll kill you."

"That's fine," Levin said with a nervous flickering smile, and he ended the call quickly to prevent himself from reversing himself.

"Everything all right?" the Chairman said.

"Oh, yes," Levin said.

But he realized that he was shaking violently.

He started to take off his coat and—alarmed that his shaking was making it impossible to do so gracefully—he became even more anxious, and dropped the coat on the floor.

The night was going badly awry.

"Are you sure you're all right?" the Chairman asked again.

"Yes, absolutely," he said, bending to retrieve his coat. "Let's sit down."

A restaurant worker who had approached to pick up the coat

from the floor now offered to check it for him—and, reluctantly, he accepted, afraid of what might occur in front of the coat-check woman if he went to check it himself.

He nodded slightly toward the coat check to convey an apology for his indisposition. There would be time later on to make things right.

Levin was now beset by manglings and chest melting of maximal intensity. It was difficult even to walk to the table, and by the time he sat down he had to wince deeply, as though to make up in one grand wince for all the smaller winces he had suppressed during the walk over. He was not unaware that he ought to wince properly—even winces can be expressions of dignity and sophistication, in the right hands—but everything was too distracting, all his thoughts were in a whirl, and he was on fire with panic at what the threatener might now do.

The Chairman took up the menu and began to flick his tongue as he read it, as though tasting each of the dishes in turn. "What's good here?" he asked.

"I . . ." Levin said, then had to stop speaking and steel himself against a new round of chest melting.

The Chairman fortunately was distracted by his lick-reading.

Levin took deep breaths and tried to reason his way back to sanity. Couldn't he count on some forbearance from the threatener? They had surely reached a level of understanding by now that allowed for the occasional tiff or misunderstanding without its causing everything to collapse . . .

And Levin would make it up to him later on; he would kowtow with extra degradation; he would set aside some of his own superiority and let the threatener have his way.

He wondered if he should somehow signal to the threatener this willingness, even a bit of regret at what he had had to do . . . But how could he do so? He didn't have the threatener's number . . .

"The steak seems promising," the Chairman said.

Levin, grimacing with new determination, decided to arrange his body no matter at what effort into a position of dignity and ease. This was a test: men under the threat of death have to contend with bouts of shaking and panic at the worst times, and continue to eat and drink in a dignified way, and he would do so.

At that moment, in the corner of his eye, he saw a figure moving toward the table at a rapid pace. Turning toward it, he saw that it was a man in a very fine tuxedo with a short flat sheen of dark hair and an expression of irked determination on his face.

He was walking with stiff, very rapid steps directly toward Levin. "Sir!" he called out.

Levin screamed.

For a moment, he thought there was nothing he could do but die—to stand up from the table seemed too difficult and complicated a task—and he screamed again as if only to pass the time until his death.

Then, with a jolt of adrenaline that propelled him, he got up and started to run as fast as he could away from the tuxedoed man. He found himself approaching a door that he assumed led to the kitchen. He had, on the way, let out a few more shrieks, which, once he gained awareness of them, he changed into cries of: "Help! Help!"

Reaching the kitchen door, he pushed into it, colliding with a waiter who was holding two dinners that smashed onto the floor.

In the kitchen, he ducked behind a counter and again cried for help.

Then there was a long, strange period of quiet. Nothing seemed to be happening; no one was coming; Levin was simply cowering in a crouch. Around him, the kitchen workers went on with restaurant business. One of them, a line cook with sharp earlobes, called out to Levin: "What are you doing." But he was so absorbed in his work, from which he did not pause or even look up, that it was clear he meant it as a statement and not a question.

Was he dead? He was fairly sure that he was not, but he could not account for this strange anticlimax. Eventually his curiosity prevailed, and he slowly made his way out from his cowering place, looked around tentatively, then walked back out of the kitchen into the dining area.

The tuxedoed man was standing in front of him.

"Your fiber supplements, sir," he said. "We found them on the floor."

The man was holding the canister with two fingers from the very top, as though it were coated with some invisible substance that he wanted to avoid touching.

"I didn't mean to startle you," he said.

Evidently only a minute had passed since he had entered the kitchen, though to Levin it had felt like much longer.

People were staring at him. An elderly couple was whispering to each other; a crag-faced man in a blue tie and thin black glasses was scratching his cheek; a portly fellow with kindly eyes was tearing a piece of bread into small bits, as though wishing not to wholly waste the time that he must now divert from eating his dinner and devote to staring.

And beyond them, somewhere, though he could not bear to confirm it, the coat-check woman . . .

A couple of restaurant workers whom Levin had never seen before had emerged from the establishment's unseen background—a man with a curled cord connecting to his ear and a woman in a smart business suit holding a clipboard. They moved with swift but impeccable precision, directing busboys who were busily cleaning up the mess that had been created by the smashed dinners. The emergence of all these unusual workers alarmed Levin. It seemed as though the machinery that would result in his expulsion from the restaurant had already begun its complex, half-hidden work.

Even in the moment of his greatest humiliation, Levin was able to marvel at the terrific sophistication of the restaurant, whose thousand moving parts, like those of a fine Swiss watch, were most of the time invisible.

12

AN HOUR LATER, ALONE AGAIN AFTER THE DINNER, HE walked and walked, in a kind of a haze, going over in his mind—in between wishes to die out of the shame that now poisoned him—the fractured memories of the remainder of the dinner, which had passed in a confused whirl. Somehow he had sat back down and eaten with the Chairman, who—out of some strange game that Levin could not begin to understand; his fatigue was now too great to unravel yet another arcane rite—had acted as if nothing unusual had happened.

But Levin could not escape the sense that he had been excommunicated from the circle of those on the higher plane. Of course, if this were so, the Chairman would not evince even a hint of it in his face. And Levin had stared, through the rest of the dinner, in absolute puzzlement at the utter blankness on that face, as though by staring long enough he could decipher the code contained in it. But it was a perfectly constructed and utterly impregnable façade of normality—one that Levin knew he could never hope to penetrate. No, it was not simply a matter of his fatigue, he suspected. He had never been meant to understand these things.

What had been clear and unmistakable, in contrast to the enigmatic ambiguity of the Chairman's face, were the joke-thinking glances of the other patrons in the restaurant—the very glances with which the lawyers on the elevator used to promise each other jokes at Levin's expense. For that is what the stares that had met him when he had come out of the kitchen had transformed themselves into once he had sat down again . . . the chin-scratching man in thin glasses, the kindly bread-tearer . . . all of them had stopped their staring only to begin instead to exchange glances full of the promise of future joke-making that was unmistakable to him in its familiarity.

Every time he diverted his gaze even for a moment from the Chairman, he could not avoid them! They came from all sides, as though not a single patron in the restaurant wished to be excluded. They were all taking care to avoid being caught—were making every effort to continue with the usual motions of their dignified eating—but the ironic glimmers in their eyes, the slight twitches of the mouth with which they previewed the laughter that would pour forth once Levin was out of sight, could not escape Levin's acute gaze.

For even if he was now to be ostracized from the higher plane of life, he had been a visitor there long enough to recognize the signs of his own judgment.

On the way out, he had shaken the Chairman's hand and had taken his coat from the coat-check woman with poisonous shame—a shame that would never leave him, unless he could expiate it through death.

Now, as he walked, he had no sense of his death-threat bearing, and—most alarming—no desire even to try to recapture it. All joy had gone out of the death threat, and he took step after aimless step with mirthless plodding.

The strangers he passed, whose magnificent ignorance of his predicament had only the day before captivated and amused him, now seemed to have been briefed on his misfortune. Everyone knew: for he had been upon the stage when the worst had happened. It wouldn't take long for word to filter to the other Melvin Levins, certainly—and oh, how they'd smirk! How they'd love to hear it! One more Melvin Levin off the books. The geologist would toast his now-unassailable victory with his slender-elbowed wife over a fine wine, that was to be expected; but with Levin out of the way, even the pharmacist in Tulsa could reasonably think he had a shot, would at least enjoy an easy night or two, and his customers would wonder with bemusement why they had received an extra smile and word of good cheer with their medications. They would have no idea what tremendous human misery had paid for that smile.

And with every few steps Levin took, there came another flash of the image of those stares in the restaurant . . . those stares and those joke-thinking glances . . .

He wished for the threatener to dismember him alive. He wished for the threatener to stab him, to burn him, to flay him as he had promised—and to do it before them all. He wished for the threatener to finally carry out all his extravagant promises which he had tossed off (Levin thought now with true contempt) with barely a thought for how he would actually fulfill them. He wished for the threatener to stab his eyes out, to boil him in acid, to rip his limbs apart, to throw him from the tops of tall buildings—and all this before the masses who had denigrated the threat, had laughed at it as though it were nothing, had appropriated the joke-thinking glances of the lawyers as though they were entitled to such glances! The sheer perversion of it enraged him.

And he would like it all to happen, too, before the coat-check woman, if only as a way of expiating the humiliation that had just occurred. Of course it was impossible. Even if the bungling threatener were able to arrange for one of these killings, how would Levin invite the coat-check woman to see it? What he really needed was a series of his own deaths, each before a different group of people, which would afford the additional convenience of allowing him to be murdered by many different methods that would not necessarily be compatible in a single killing.

The idea was laughable, given the incompetence of the threatener.

Since he couldn't be killed, he needed to find some other way to disperse this overpowering shame—to eliminate the unending recurrence of those terrible, terrible stares. He walked and walked, hoping to shake the shame off by the force of his movement, but it had attached itself to him like a stench.

If he couldn't shake off his shame, he wished at least to shake off his drunkenness, which was becoming a greater and greater encumbrance to his walking.

After a long time of wandering, he arrived at his office building. Once again, his feet had carried him somewhere of their own accord. As a man under the threat of death, he had become accustomed to trusting that these automatic wanderings took him to destinations that possessed a certain significance. Immediately he decided that he must apply this faith even still—even in spite of whatever had become of him.

He went in and took the elevator up to the fourth floor.

Emptied of workers and only dimly lit, the office was pervaded by an eerie stillness. What use he could have made of an eerie stillness only a few hours before! To be a man threatened by death amid the eerie stillness of a deserted office . . . it was a thought whose deliciousness now stung Levin with the regret of an unfulfilled promise.

How he could have slunk around, taking in the delicious essence of that mysteriousness! How he could have soaked in it!

And why couldn't he now slink—why couldn't he now soak? Wasn't he still a man under the threat of death?

But he knew that things of that kind were irretrievably behind him.

The lawyers, who kept late hours, were no doubt up there on nine right now, lawyering away, but he could take no comfort in their presence—their tantalizing proximity now seemed only to reinforce his separateness from them. The thought that he could in a few minutes be among them was newly poisonous to him. Yesterday, if he had done it, if he had gone up and asked them all to an impromptu drink—yes, he might have dared it then!—they would have acceded; they would have shared all their elevator anecdotes, initiated him into their club. But now he couldn't even think of it. Even if they had not yet heard, through their sophisticated channels, something of what had happened at the restaurant, then they would read it in his face, in his bearing; they would take one look at him, clam up in their lawyerly way, and later, as soon as he had left, turn to one another and say, "Something happened at the restaurant."

To think, he had not even bothered to approach the lawyers while he still could. How he'd wasted everything! A threat, and all the possibilities such a thing had offered—he had flushed it all away, just like everything else.

But then it wasn't all his fault. The threatener—with his blunders and his uncultivated style—had put Levin in an untenable position. Having to juggle such an incompetent threatener had frayed Levin's nerves too much, pushed him too far—as it would anyone. He could not be blamed for reacting as he had. It said nothing about *him* . . .

He had come to Flemingson's cubicle. The sight of it reminded him of the promotion, Adderley's position, and the presentation which he had eschewed—a thought that now filled him with profound regret. The promotion, which he had written off as irrelevant after the threat had imbued his existence with a far more important dimension, he now saw with clarity was in fact all-important, the only thing he should have been obsessed with—for the threat had proved a false promise, its window onto the vista of a new life merely a mirage.

Centered among the porcelain animal figurines was a cluster forming a new scene. It was possible that Flemingson had staged it after work today, after the others had left, ready for its debut tomorrow—or that it had been there for several days and Levin, enwrapped as he had been in his own pressing concerns, had been unaware of it.

It showed a lone dog looking toward an enclosed circle of cats.

Levin had always made fun of the animal scenes, smiling to himself at their inanity. Now, for the first time, he saw the pathos in one of them. In a flash he saw the plight of the lone dog, shunned and unacknowledged by all those pitiless cats, and he felt a surge of sadness.

Among Flemingson's other knickknacks was a miniature novelty baseball bat. Levin picked up this bat absent-mindedly and started running his hands over its wooden surface.

He eyed the dog. The emotion that it had evoked was becoming confused. He pitied it, it was true—but at the same time he disdained it. And he disdained, too, Flemingson, for putting the dog there—and also admired him for the cunning of it. And it was all connected, somehow, with the threatener, for whose negligence and incompetence he felt such uncontainable resentment, the threatener who should have been his equal, the threatener with whom he should have been locked in battle till the end of one of their days!

Somewhere amid the confusion was also a notion that he vaguely recalled had been helpful to him in the previous days, which was that he should, as a man under the threat of death—above all—not simply think, but act.

And he brought the bat down upon the porcelain dog with all his might.

Smashing it felt interesting. Along with the figurine, he had also fractured reality as he'd always known it, and exposed a new dimension of existence—one in which he had smashed a figurine on Flemingson's desk. There was something unreal about it, something dreamlike—and yet there was a charge to it, too, not dissimilar from the vibrations caused by his earlier acts of boldness. Here was yet another species of boldness. Here was yet another sloughing off of his previous, faulty self.

The subsequent smashes were done as much to plumb this strange new feeling as to actually accomplish more smashing. Though more smashing was accomplished—much more. He soon became aware that there was a wasteland of porcelain shards that stretched across Flemingson's whole desk, and only two or three intact figurines remaining amid the wreckage.

And for some reason it seemed almost a duty to complete the smashing with half a dozen joyless, perfunctory strokes.

13

HE AWOKE THE NEXT MORNING IN PAIN. THE ACT OF smashing had exacerbated his back injury terribly, and he couldn't help but resent his back doctor for not warning him, "Be careful about smashing motions."

Delicately, he sat up in bed to see whether he felt himself once again to be a man under the threat of death, a man on the higher plane of life. It was as though he were waiting for a verdict, and he did so with some impatience.

But all he felt was a kind of inner deadness, an overpowering lethargy, which, combined with the flaring back pains, was enormously unpleasant.

In the bathroom, dazed and aching, he tried to reattain the sense of himself as a man under the threat of death in the way that had once been so effective. He leaned toward the mirror, and, whispering to himself again and again that he was a man under the threat of death, rearranged his expression into some of its most dignified forms, pursing his lips and wrinkling his forehead. But all of these previously reliable methods were now, it was obvious, hopeless. He felt only as though he were constructing something by rote—trying something on rather than really inhabiting it.

He wished he had taken video of himself earlier in the week, when he had been glowing with dignity, so that he could now study it. But even this, he knew on some deep level, would have been useless—for all the study in the world couldn't make up for what must flow naturally from deeply hidden wells within oneself.

Had he never really had it? Had it all been an illusion?

He ate his breakfast and then walked to Mrs. Cohen's door to deliver her fiber supplements.

"They're the wrong kind," she said.

"It can't be," Levin said, but then he looked and saw that she was right. "Well, I've been distracted by a threat," he said.

"Oh, that's all right," Mrs. Cohen said.

Back in his apartment, he sat before his threat items. Centered among them was the initial note, the one that had set it all off, which now had a historical air about it. It seemed to come from a distant era, a life separate from his own. ". . . You'll be flayed," he read, with a certain wistfulness. How stunned he had been by those words!

He closed his eyes and tried to see himself receiving the threat, contending with it, all the stages through which he had passed— walking through mysterious, rain-soaked streets; engaging in a *pas de deux* with the threatener; bent in deep study over the threat's innumerable puzzles. He had no connection to these events now. And when he tried to concentrate on these images more intensely, to try to inhabit them, the twin images of the night before—of his humiliation at the restaurant and of his smashing the animals— would intrude, dissolving everything else.

But then he had an idea. He was not, perhaps, a man on the higher plane of life—but he was, he realized, a man who smashed figurines. And that, he felt with a hint of something wild awakening in him, was a thing not without significance. A man who, in an office after hours, late at night, smashes the figurines of a colleague—a man who, having lost everything, now lives his life with heedless abandon.

A man, in other words, who is capable of anything.

This idea pleased him—briefly. He was unable to catch hold of it for more than a moment. He thought to himself again: *a man capable of anything*—and, having bestowed this designation upon himself, he went back to the mirror to see if he could inhabit it.

He stared at himself, imagined again the smashing of the figurines, and compressed his face into a vicious scowl. When this proved insufficient, he briefly growled, stopped to look around out of the irrational fear that his growling might have been heard, then turned back to the mirror and growled a bit more.

He could feel the wildness in him, if not fully awakening, then at least beginning to stir.

He left for work. In the hall, he saw Mrs. Cohen again. She was taking up her mail. She smiled at him and told him not to worry about the fiber supplements.

He responded only with a smile almost devoid of friendliness—in keeping with the nihilism that was now propelling him.

Then, passing the mail room, he glanced at a package addressed to the exerciser. With contempt, he kicked it, and not gently.

For he was dangerous now—a man capable of anything.

The new post-smashing air of the office hit him as soon as he entered. There was a morgue-like quiet. Everyone was gathered around the crime scene. None of the shards had been touched, though it was clear from the way that everyone was posed—in bereft contemplation—that this was less out of forensic necessity than a certain sense of holiness which should not be disturbed.

Flemingson himself was frozen in a pose of deep contemplation, his downward-inclined head poised on both fists and his brow furrowed, as though he had hastily studied *The Thinker* and missed the key detail of the single hand.

Around him was a tableau of sympathy such as never could have been imagined—a new masterpiece. A woman from HR was openly weeping; her sob seemed to contain two distinct tones that violinically formed the perfect dissonance, and she would look up now and again from her sobs and shake her head at the ceiling as though baying at a deity.

Dennis, the skeptic, was standing with his head bowed, as though in acknowledgment that, while he could not curtail his look of skepticism, he did not wish for it to be seen in these circumstances.

Leonard was uncharacteristically staid, his tongue kept in as if out of respect. "We'll figure out who did this," he kept saying, but quietly, a nod to the enthusiasm that was brewing within him but that would not be permitted to develop fully until the appropriate time.

For Flemingson, everyone instinctively found the proper aesthetic and adhered to it without erring.

Only Meldon was absent.

One of the figurines had survived, a penguin, and the group was talking about it as though it were some kind of miracle of divine mercy. Levin was astonished, too, for his own reasons. How could he have missed it? He had to suppress the impulse to offer to smash it, as if out of politeness.

"I just don't see how it could have happened . . ." Flemingson said.

The violinic sobbing continued, while a couple other people complimented Flemingson on this comment.

Levin was about to go up to Flemingson and offer his own perfunctory condolences, as a matter of good form. But then, remembering that he was now a man capable of anything, a man leaving in his wake a trail of nihilistic chaos, he decided to put on an expression of facetious glee—as though he found the whole thing funny and was only suppressing his laughter out of a grudging concession to propriety—and even considered simply going to his own desk without a word of acknowledgment of the smashing.

He compromised by offering Flemingson an incredibly brief word of consolation.

Marla approached Levin with a strange look on her face. It was scrunched into what seemed to Levin to be irony, or almost complicity. He had the sense that he was about to be let in on a secret.

A hope rose within him. Could it be? Was she going to tell him some undermining fact—that they were all secretly glad of the smashing? That they knew, in the midst of this charade, who the real sufferer was? That a death threat, though borne with such equanimity that no one could guess at the unseen toll it takes, makes smashings seem by comparison like nothing more than a stubbed toe? Marla, of all people—could she be the one to show him that there was hope left in the world?

If she asked about the threat, he owed it to her not to tell her what had happened—to assure her that it was escalating still, that he was still facing those escalations with courage and dignity, that it certainly had not led to any humiliations.

And he decided on the spot that he would say he had received a small dead animal preserved in formaldehyde but that it was not shaking his spirits in the slightest.

Marla leaned toward him to whisper: "Do you have the napkins?"

The nihilistic glee within him surged back.

"I forgot them," he said, with a smile which he imagined to be terrifying.

Marla frowned. "Well, there's still time."

Levin reacted with silence, giving off only a little wince.

But she was deaf to winces. "They just have to be here by six, that's all."

This was now to be his fate, he supposed—to pick up napkins for people who could not read gestures that were as clear as signposts.

Meldon emerged from his office with an air of solemnity, making motions that signaled coming oratory. Everyone quieted down, and Meldon announced that he was awarding the promotion to Flemingson.

There was no applause—but only out of respect for the solemnity of the occasion; the satisfaction and approbation of everyone was perfectly conveyed.

The news of the promotion threw Levin off a bit. He remembered that, as a man under the threat of death, he did not care about the promotion. He began to adjust his expression to show that, given the loftier concerns that occupied him, the promotion was so irrelevant as to be beneath even mockery—an expression that involved pitching his eyebrows high up on his forehead and zig-zagging his head in nods which were meant to be sarcastic—but then, remembering that he was also now a man capable of anything, a dangerous man, he re-lowered his eyebrows and started to scowl.

His expressions were becoming confused, and so too were the aspects and modes of his being.

"So the party tonight will really be for Adderley *and* Flemingson," Meldon went on. "We'll fit two in the box, as it were."

"That means you should get extra napkins," Marla told Levin, illogically.

He spent the day in a deeply uncomfortable daze. His fatigue was unrelenting, his head was pounding, and his state of being was still a hopeless confusion. The nihilistic glee that he had discovered in the morning was present at times; for a moment it would animate him, and he would clench his fists and spread a wild and devious smile across his face, amazed at the force of this anger—but then it would recede behind the deadening fatigue that was muting everything, and he would again become confused and weakened. He made the hours pass, one after another, in this exhausting suffering.

And then the end of the day was not really the end of the day, but only a kind of break before the next misery—Adderley's party—was to commence. He got up to go get the napkins. At least this idiotic task would allow him to leave for a bit. Perhaps he had a chance of reassembling his being outside the office.

On his way out, Meldon pulled him aside. "I just want to tell you that the Chairman had an excellent time at dinner," he said. "Well done."

While walking to the napkin store, he had the thought that if he could cackle at the absurdity of everything—of the whole confusion that his life had become, but in particular the absurdity of his walking to get napkins for the party—it would do him much good, perhaps restore him completely. He even opened his mouth as though to begin the cackles, but he was too self-conscious to continue. A blush of shame came over him, for he was now someone afraid even to cackle. He knew that the Chairman likely seldom or never had occasion to cackle, but that if he somehow did he would let the cackles loose with the same unthinking abandon of his incredible nose-blowing honk.

The party store was full of running children. Levin approached the counter. The attendant was a large-haired woman who was chewing gum rapidly as though it were an urgent task. Levin had no patience for napkin shenanigans. He plopped his hands on the counter in a jarring tap.

"I need yellow and purple napkins, and I'm told you have a . . ."—and he sighed, resentful of his own fluency in the matter—"a cat design."

"Did you want the Cheshire cat or the black cat?"

Levin frowned. "Either."

She tapped into her computer. "We only have the Cheshire cat left."

"Then the Cheshire cat."

She tapped more at the computer, and then said, "But we don't have them in purple and yellow."

Levin's phone rang, and he answered. "What!" he said sharply. It was the wheezy voice of the threatener. "Hello."

"We could order from another store," the clerk said.

"Are you ready for your next odyssey?" the threatener said.

"What?"

"Your next odyssey."

"You're giving me another odyssey? That's it? No punishment for my defiance?"

"Sir?" the clerk said, as though impatient at Levin's distraction.

Levin glanced at the clerk, piqued. "I'm on the phone!"

The clerk stopped chewing her gum, evidently as an expression of shock at Levin's rudeness.

"What defiance?" the threatener said.

"I didn't do the last odyssey! I hung up in your face!"

"Oh."

"'Oh?' 'Oh?'" Levin said, furious. He felt that now, with his fury at the threatener, he had finally gained a firm hold of the nihilism inside of him. Seizing this opportunity to strengthen his grip on it as much as he could—to stoke the wildness and bring it to a blaze—he said it a couple more times: "'Oh?' 'Oh?'"

Then he went on: "I defy you, and all you have for me is an 'oh'?!"

"Or we could do fuchsia, it looks like," the clerk said, chewing away once again.

"Fuchsia?" Levin said.

"What?" said the threatener.

"That wasn't for you."

"Or I could order them," the clerk was saying, "and you'll have them in two days."

Levin's anger was overpowering. "Why don't you just go ahead and kill me!" he said loudly.

"What?"

Levin was momentarily frightened by what he had said. But—realizing that in order to seal his status as a dangerous man capable of anything, he had to continue on this path—he said it again: "Kill me, I said!"

The napkin salesperson was looking at him aghast, but with brash indifference Levin merely walked out of the store.

"Okay, I will," the threatener was saying.

"No, you won't."

"What?"

"You won't kill me. You never were going to kill me. You're too cowardly."

"That's not true."

"It *is* true! You threaten and threaten—but you never meant a word of it. I never thought you did!" Levin's goading was having a terrific revitalizing effect on his spirit. It was as though, with each goad, he were injecting a bit of energy into his body. "I never thought for a second that you'd kill me! I never thought for a second that the threat was genuine!"

"I *will* kill you," the threatener said matter-of-factly, as though correcting someone who mistakenly believes it is not raining.

"Then do it!" Levin yelled. "I'm on my way to my office right now! We're having a ceremony for Adderley! I'm sure you had no idea of that! I'm sure you have no idea of my comings and goings—not the faintest clue of my schedule! You probably have never even followed me anywhere!"

After waiting a bit and getting nothing but silence, Levin continued, becoming more and more crazed.

"You probably don't even know where my office is, do you! Do you!"

After a pause, the threatener admitted that he did not.

And Levin in a bout of spiteful fury shrieked the address

into the phone, followed by the security code for entrance after hours.

"So come kill me if you want. Come kill me, you coward."

"Fine, I will."

Levin felt a small rush of fear at this statement—but it dissipated quickly back into the crazed anger that was powering him.

"Great! Don't forget to bring your knife!" Levin said sarcastically.

"I won't."

Levin's manner now changed abruptly. Suddenly he saw the prospect of his death before him once again, and, as though he were a car salesman who has given up on a customer only to realize he has one last chance to make the sale, he began to speak with more purpose and seriousness. He felt he now had one final chance to forestall the threatener's incompetence.

"Really don't forget to bring your knife," he said, with sober purpose.

"I won't."

"Double check, okay? And actually, do you have a gun?"

"Yes."

"Maybe use that instead. And think very hard about any other supplies you might need. Really think it through."

"I have everything."

"Walk yourself through the whole thing and make a list of anything you'll need for each stage. And what are you going to wear?"

"What?"

Wincing at what he might be preventing, Levin said, "Just make yourself presentable."

Levin hung up, and, vibrating with a strange amalgam of anger, determination, mirth, and terror, he walked to the office as fast as he could, as though not to allow himself too much time to think.

He seemed to have engineered his own murder—a thought that momentarily frightened him. But, as he walked—with rapid, irregular steps that caused his surroundings to sway drunkenly around him—he found his contempt for the threatener's incompetence leaching into his body, further and further dissolving his fear. Of course the threatener would never show. He was a nonentity—an embarrassment to everyone who has ever called himself a threatener—and Levin had, by practically inviting him to the party and giving him such explicit instructions to guard against his incompetence, found the perfect joke to play on the situation. For a moment, he was able to smile at this joke—before his contempt for the threatener again escalated into overpowering anger, and he found himself once again cursing that hopeless incompetence, hoping against all odds that the threatener *would* in fact come to kill him, wondering if he should even call him to make sure he knew the way to the office—before realizing that this was ridiculous, since he had no way of calling the threatener.

It was a volatile and confusing walk, and he had been standing at the door to his office building for some time without realizing it when Marla arrived.

"Have the napkins?" she asked.

She was furious that he did not, and, once they were in the office and the party had begun, was not shy about showing it. She sulked in a corner—Levin was sure he saw her in at least two different corners sulking, and puffing out her cheeks in anger, as though she were making her way to all the corners for the purpose—and would from time to time make a glancing remark about the inadequacy of the white napkins that were stocked already in the office and that they had been forced to use, handing someone their food and saying, "Just take one of the white napkins," as she eyed Levin with murderous contempt.

The party was insufferable. There was pizza and endless

chit-chat. Leonard reminisced about an earlier enthusiasm concerning a certain small-town murder years before. Flemingson, after vowing that they would have to wait until the next day to see his next figurine—the first of his new collection—finally relented and showed them, briefly, a porcelain leopard.

Adderley himself, the man of honor, shriveled and shrunken in his huge suit as though the result of a botched magic trick that had been meant to make him disappear but had only gone halfway, had been positioned in a place of some prominence on his scooter and remained stationary.

Levin all the while waited with tremendous discomfort to see what would happen. It was hard to say if the unpleasant feeling he was experiencing was simply the unpleasantness of being at a party of his coworkers, or that of the possibility of being murdered. The latter thought had a way of startling him, and from time to time a huge rush of unbelievable disquiet came over him, causing for a moment the whole world to fade out and a really disconcerting new reality to take over everything, an incredible and highly uncomfortable feeling, as though for one second he could see that he had fallen from the top of a skyscraper and was hurtling toward the pavement at terminal velocity—but then he was back amid the merely ordinary unpleasantness of the party.

Shouldn't he tell them? Wasn't that the rational thing to do— to tell them the threatener was on his way? To prepare them for this final confrontation so that they would have a chance of stopping it?

But no, he thought with a scowl: he was wise to that game. That is just what the threatener wanted. Levin would alert them all, make a big show of it, put everyone in hiding places to rush the threatener when he came in—only for him never to show, thereby reducing Levin to dispensing shrugging apologies as he brought them out of their hiding places one by one, taking in their looks of indulgent sympathy that would not conceal—for these rubes knew nothing about concealing sentiments—their doubt that the threat had ever been real at all.

Then Levin was furious again, and he prayed for the threatener to come, to come quickly, to shoot him in the head before them all—an image that in turn frightened him.

But of course he would not come.

Marla was going around with an envelope, soliciting contributions for a fund to replace Flemingson's smashed figurines.

Levin, who didn't have any cash, apologized to Flemingson.

"It was going to be a surprise!" Marla screamed at him.

And where was the threatener? Where was the angel of his death? Late, of course. If he were even coming at all, which surely he was not.

Then it was time for the speeches.

"Should we have cake first?" someone suggested.

"We'll need more napkins," said Marla. "Unfortunately, there are only white ones, in the supply room."

Levin, on the point of telling her that they could use his clothes as napkins once he was dead, which would be very soon, instead said, "I'll get them."

In the supply room he was so absorbed in finding the napkins that it took him several seconds to notice that there was a man crouched next to a stack of papers.

And yet another moment had to pass before he realized that the man was holding a gun.

14

EVIN FROZE. HIS FIRST IMPULSE WAS TO SIMPLY WALK out as if he hadn't noticed anything, though he also had an impulse to apologize. He felt as though he had accidentally intruded on someone changing their clothes.

Then he began to tremble uncontrollably.

"Are you the threatener?" he asked.

"Yes," the gun-holding man said.

So here was the threatener. No wonder he wheezed, no wonder his voice always sounded distant and frail! The latent gravelliness that it promised had always been nothing more than an illusion, Levin realized. For the threatener was a wrinkled, bald old man, easily in his sixties. And he was tiny. And not a tininess that conceals cagey violence, but a merely diminutive tininess. Levin felt he could knock the threatener over without too much effort. He was wearing huge, thin-framed glasses which added to the geriatric effect, and they sat on a face that was—there was no other way to say it—friendly. He had a thin, scraggly beard that enhanced the aura of friendliness and weakness, and a large mole on the lower part of his left cheek, which for some reason Levin found especially annoying.

It was a face that was all wrong for a threatener. Levin was enormously disappointed. All his hours imagining a suave, sophisticated threatener, all the care with which he had appointed the threatener's lair and bestowed state-of-the-art tools on him—all a complete waste of time.

"And now I'm going to kill you," the threatener wheezed.

"What were you doing in here?" Levin said.

"I was going to jump out," said the threatener.

"When?!" groaned Levin. "*When* were you going to jump out?"

The threatener scratched his chin instead of answering.

Levin exhaled, squeezing his fists in frustration, then turned his gaze to the gun, which was shaking in the threatener's hands. The threatener had placed his left hand underneath the right gun-holding hand as a kind of pedestal, as though he were too weak to hold it with one hand, creating a ridiculous effect.

Nevertheless, the gun, pointed at Levin, was—and this, Levin realized with a shattering clarity, was the crucial thing—perfectly capable of going off, killing him. Levin could see that now.

So he was going to be killed. That fact was before him now, in all its stark and gray reality, and he shrugged his shoulders at it, as at all the other matter-of-fact developments in his matter-of-fact life. The fact that he was going to be killed now seemed no more monumental or menacing than any of the other prosaic realizations that had studded the lackluster progress that had brought him to this moment, and he saw all at once how senseless all his wild rushes of fear had been. To be murdered was no more or less remarkable than not getting the promotion. It was true that he was shaking almost violently. But the shaking was entirely incidental: it had no relationship to his affective state, which was close to null; also it seemed in a sense to be canceled out by the threatener's own shaking, as though shaking were simply the rule for this room.

And they stood there facing each other, two shaking men, one with a gun trained on the other, as though it were a satisfactory situation that neither saw any reason to alter.

Death had now come as the result of a series of miscalculations he had made since receiving the threat. And it would be a fitting death, as everyone would be able to see at once. "He was killed by a trembling, tiny man," they would say. "Don't forget the mole," someone—probably Leonard, with his mania for completeness—would add.

Then there was the fact that he was going to be killed in a supply closet. Levin looked around at the unopened reams of paper, the cardboard boxes of supplies, the filing cabinets crowded together in such a way that it was unclear if the cabinets contained items that were being stored or were themselves being stored. He couldn't hear anything of the party at all; it was possible they were playing music and even conceivable they would not hear the gunshot. Here is where he would be found—very possibly the next morning by the custodial staff—and cleared away without a trace.

And outside, just beyond the door, were all the callous rubes who would be spared the sight of his killing . . .

"What about a final request?" Levin said suddenly.

"Huh?" said the threatener.

Levin was almost annoyed that he now had to contend with one last desire. But there it was: he wished to move the proceedings to the main office. He would be killed before them all, as he had intended, and would thereby transform Flemingson's greatest tableau of sympathy into his own—his final revenge.

"Would you grant me a final request? Before I die?" Levin asked again.

"What is it?"

"Take me outside. And hold me hostage and kill me in front of them."

"No, I don't like it," the threatener said after a pause of deliberation. "Too dangerous." He had the air of a dimwit arriving at a conclusion to which he has been carefully guided.

"Are you kidding? None of them has any weapons, and certainly no courage. They will look on and do nothing." Levin felt a surge of glee at the thought. "They'll let me be killed as though they were watching a movie. You have my word of honor on that."

"I'm not sure," the threatener said, though it was obvious from his hesitation that the game was won. Levin now simply had to execute the mate. He realized this with some resentment. He had become expert at manipulating the threatener, a sad fact that spoke as much to the threatener's incompetence, Levin acknowledged with bitterness, as to his own cleverness. Even his spectacular death was to be diminished by the threatener's utter and unconcealable unfitness.

"Okay," the threatener said, predictably.

Now they faced each other, still trembling, and for a moment neither knew how to or wished to take the next step.

The sight of the threatener's mole finally caused Levin to take the initiative.

"Do you have to hold the gun like that?" he said.

"That's how I was taught."

"You should tie me up," Levin said. He was, in the sudden frantic desire to get everything right, jumping from one thing to another without any organization, but it could not be helped.

They tried to find some rope to tie him up with, but nothing was suitable.

"Forget it," Levin said. "You'll hold me, you'll get me into some kind of nelson—can you do that?"

"Yes." The threatener was scratching his chin again, apparently a nervous habit.

"Don't scratch your chin so much when we're out there."

"All right."

Levin looked with distress at the threatener's unruly beard and haircut, then glanced around the supply room in a half-hearted attempt to find some implements to fix them, but of course there was nothing. For a supply room, it was totally bare of implements with which to prepare a dignified killing.

"Do it quickly," Levin said, and, feeling a resurgence of fear, looked again at the threatener's mole, which dissipated it. "Do it relatively quickly, no long speeches or anything." Levin could only imagine what embarrassments might come of the threatener orating.

The threatener began to hiccup.

"What's that?" Levin asked.

"What?"

"You're hiccupping?"

"I guess so."

They stood for a while, waiting for the hiccups to stop.

"How long does it usually take?"

"Only a few minutes," the threatener said.

To his credit, this proved accurate. When the hiccups had finished, Levin allowed the threatener to place him into a hold, and they began to move toward the door. The gun was digging uncomfortably into his back. Levin could do nothing but think of what might go wrong, and particularly the dissatisfying nature of the threatener's shabby haircut and overall appearance. He could not fully rid himself of the thought that he should call it off now, make a last-second plea—not for the sake of sparing his life, but so that they could both take more time to prepare. But he knew of course that the threatener would never accede to such a crazy request—and Levin took a touch of satisfaction in the fact that he could not now go back if he wished, that he had set the machine of his own demise incontrovertibly in motion.

When they came to the door, Levin had attained a state of almost transcendent acceptance. He had an impulse to turn to the threatener, to shake his hand (he would have to ask him to loosen his hold for the shaking, but felt that would not be a problem) or at least make some kind of valedictory remark—something to mark the end of their long, fraught, intense relationship.

But in an instant they were through the door, before everyone.

They were eating cake, evidently without the benefit of the napkins that Levin had been sent to retrieve. Meldon had begun the first speech. He was well into a box metaphor. And no one noticed that Levin had emerged from the closet with a gun at his back.

"Ahem," Levin said quietly.

"The hinges are in a sense the most important element," Meldon said.

Levin turned to the threatener. "You need to say it."

"Say what?"

Levin frowned. "Hey, everyone," he said, loudly.

They finally turned. Meldon grimaced slightly at being interrupted. Everyone was staring dumbly, and Levin realized that they could not actually see the gun.

"You have to turn me," he said to the threatener.

The threatener turned him with an awkward motion, digging his thumb into Levin's ribs annoyingly as he did it, until the gun was partially visible to everyone.

This elicited a few satisfying gasps. Everyone froze, their cake slices held aloft. Dennis's slice had his fork stuck in it like a flag of conquest.

"Nobody move or say a word, or I'll kill him," the threatener said.

"Oh my God!" Marla then said, as though to hasten Levin's death by expressly not following directions.

"He said not to speak," Levin said angrily.

There was another silence, and Levin was transported back to the phone calls during which he had had to drag every bit from the threatener with excruciating effort. "Tell them . . ." he coaxed, quietly, and then, realizing this would be useless, he continued at a more theatrical level, "you've threatened me with death, right? For over a week?"

"Yes, that's right."

The threatener began to cough. Levin grew concerned, as the coughing continued and developed into a full-blown fit, that someone was going to use the opportunity to take action, to tackle the threatener or otherwise intervene. He eyed the onlookers with trepidation, as though he could prevent a tackling with this eyeing. For a moment he considered doing the tackling himself, not out of a wish to live but only to forestall the others, and he even began to take account of which muscles he would need to activate to break free of the threatener's grip—which in truth would not be very difficult—but the coughing fit came to a close, fortunately, before Levin could contemplate this unpleasant option for very long.

But then another silence prevailed.

Was Levin to be made to discharge the gun himself? He was trapped in another impossible dilemma—he needed for the threatener to kill him without his appearing to demand it. Once again they had reached a stalemate.

At every moment, too, he was checking to see if he was still alive, or if the mysterious business of death had begun.

It was a highly unpleasant and seemingly unending state of anxiety and impatience.

Suddenly Leonard spoke: "Don't do it!"

"What's that?" the threatener said.

"Don't do it," Leonard said. "Let him go."

"How dare you," the threatener said. "I'll kill him! I'll kill him right now!"

Levin felt an overwhelming gratitude to Leonard for provoking the threatener. It was clear that this was now the way to death, and Leonard, bless his heart, had found it!

Then Flemingson spoke. "You don't want to do this."

Everyone turned to Flemingson; something in the quiet force of his voice compelled this. Even the threatener, Levin could feel by the way he adjusted his grip, had been drawn in by Flemingson's interruption in a way that he had not been by Leonard's.

"Stop now and we'll make sure you get the help you need," Flemingson said.

Levin could feel the gun slacken imperceptibly against his back.

"You have better options," Flemingson went on. "You are a better man than this. You are a better human being. And we will make sure the world can see that."

Now the gun slid downward on Levin's back more perceptibly, perhaps by an inch or two. He was astonished. How could the threatener be so weak! A whole life of threatening, and he was ready to give it up after one stupid maudlin speech from Flemingson!

"If you start negotiating with Flemingson, you'll end up regretting it," Levin said quietly through gritted teeth.

"You can choose a better path!" Flemingson said. He had found the right register for his purpose, a kind of high-pitched evangelical haranguing.

"He won't follow through," Levin mumbled.

Flemingson stepped forward cautiously, his hands held out beseechingly, his lips narrowing as though he were—against all odds and sense—going to whistle.

Instead, he said: "Here, give me the gun . . ."

Miraculously, something in the threatener hardened just then. The gun reattained its earlier position and dug into Levin's back with a delightfully sharp pain as the threatener launched into a tirade: "Everyone step back! Step back! I'm going to kill him right now before all of you, and if you intervene I'll kill the rest of you, too!"

The threatener, it had to be said, came through when necessary. It was his finest moment. His cough was now a distant memory.

And now death was coming. Levin, a pleasant dizziness coming over him, took in all the astonished glances of his coworkers. No one was chewing cake now; the botched intervention from

Flemingson—how delicious the thought of it!—had changed the mood decisively to what it should have been all along. Now it was somber and charged with unmistakable terror and pity. He had achieved, at last, the tableau of sympathy to which he had been entitled for so long. Across the room he could see Sophie, the customer-service rep, with her glassy sympathetic eyes that, widened beyond their greatest previous widening (so it seemed to Levin, peering out from the abyss into which he was sweetly sinking), were now trained on him, the masterpiece of her sympathy, its apotheosis . . .

Levin felt a profound calm. He was ready to die.

"Enjoy your rocks in hell," the threatener said, cocking the gun.

"Wait!" Leonard called out. "Just wait a minute!"

"What now?" the threatener said.

"Let him kill me," Levin said, with a warning look in his eyes.

"Did you say 'rocks'?" Leonard said with urgency.

"Yes."

"I've been doing some research on this," Leonard said, his tongue swelling and protruding in the obvious beginnings of an enthusiasm. He began to pace, forgetting the situation and the inappropriateness of pacing in it. But the confidence he had in what he was about to say—or the fullness of his enthusiasm—distracted him from such proprieties. "It turns out—you may be unaware of this—but there is another Melvin Levin who is a prominent geologist!"

The threatener turned to Levin. "You're not a geologist?" he asked.

Levin closed his eyes as tightly as he could. He saw now in an instant the collapse of everything, and he was almost offended that he still had to undergo the laborious steps that would complete it.

"I'm not," Levin had to admit.

"I've been meaning to threaten a Melvin Levin who is a geologist!"

When Levin opened his eyes, he saw Leonard standing upright

and grinning widely, as though it were the grin he had been working toward his entire life, in all of his enthusiasms, and he now
wished for it to be displayed on a pedestal.

Levin then scrutinized the threatener's friendly face, thinking
that his last hope—a slim one—was that it was some kind of joke
the threatener was playing, a final joke before death.

"Is this a joke?" Levin asked.

"No!" the threatener said. He had a look of delighted astonishment, as at running into a neighbor in some faraway place. "I've
had the wrong Melvin Levin all along! I'm so sorry."

Levin was furious. "But how could you have made a mistake
like this?" he demanded. "How is it possible? The geologist's picture is all over the internet! You could have taken one look, and
you'd know you had the wrong guy!"

"I don't know," the threatener said.

No one was sure what to do. The threatener had released Levin
and was scratching his chin, looking around as though for a cue—the
gun in his other hand hanging limply at his waist, as though it were
the leash of a well-behaved dog to whom one needn't pay attention.

"Aren't you going to make your escape?" Levin asked bitterly.

"Yes," the threatener said, and he proceeded to walk out rapidly
while once or twice—no doubt in an effort to prevent them from calling the police or trying to stop him—waving the gun perfunctorily in
a ridiculous arc, as though to swat away flies with it.

He was an embarrassment to the very end.

"Are you all right?" Marla had come up to Levin and touched
his elbow. The others were coming over as well, slowly, converging
into a tableau of sympathy that by its origin was an intolerable
sacrilege. Levin made an exaggerated motion of breaking free of
them and walked quickly to the exit without a word.

The others—thinking perhaps that he meant to chase the
threatener—did not follow.

15

H E WALKED HOME AT A RAPID PACE, THOUGH NOT
overly so, as though his shame were something he was bal-
ancing precariously, which he must get out of sight as quickly as
possible but also take care not to spill on the way.

But at home there was nothing for him: no relief from the
shame, and nothing to do at all. Without the threat he had nothing but emptiness. He sat down, got up again, walked around the
room, lay down on the bed, even fell asleep for a time—trying to
find the position that would allow him to step back into his life,
but to no avail. Hours passed; he fell asleep again; he became confused; he would wake up and think at once that he ought to work
on the threat, then remember with a shock of pain that there was
no threat, that there would never be a threat again.

What was there to do now? Kill himself. Yes, he thought with
a devilish grin—he should do what the threatener could not. It
was a wild and delicious joke, a bit of nonsense, and, his grin widening, he repeated it to himself: "I'll kill myself."

And suddenly, hearing the phrase aloud, he found a new note
of seriousness in it, and he looked up, quiet and grave.

For if he were to kill himself, then surely it would be talked
about for some time.

Now he was struck with something of the same mixture of
anxiety and profoundness that had marked his first encounters
with the threat. The air had changed again in the room. He got
up and began to pace with excitement. Wild thoughts coursed

through him as he paced, and his pacing became wilder to suit them. His suicide, in these circumstances, would make for a news story, perhaps even a national one—and all at once it would seem that the farce the threat had turned out to be was no farce at all, but merely one hint in a complicated and highly mysterious story the true dimensions of which no one had access to. He made his way around the room, his eyes fixing on things that could be used as implements of his self-destruction, but his vision was filled instead with images of the shocked puzzlement that would greet the news of his death.

"Stop your damn walking! It's two in the morning!" It was his downstairs neighbor banging on the door.

"Sorry," Levin said, an otherworldly grin coming over his face.

And he continued his suicide brainstorming with quieter steps but with no less excitement.

Suddenly his eyes fell upon the window. He stared at it, as though examining a pile of gold that lay in the corner of the room which he had only now noticed. The window, he realized, was the threshold to death: simply stepping through it was all that was required; and it was as though outside of it was not his prosaic view of the street, but the abyss, the other world, the end of everything, hovering there in the air.

He walked up to the window slowly, with fixed attention. He peered outside at the view with which he was so familiar—at the street which now seemed like a stage that had been set for decades in preparation for one grand show: his death.

He stood taller. Excited as he was, he must not forget to approach this final task with the sobriety and seriousness that it called for. For he was now a suicide—a designation that, properly understood, possessed a dignity of its own.

He made his way to the bathroom mirror where he had so often adjusted his expressions. The names of great suicides flashed

through his mind as he brought to his face the expression of appropriate graveness. He felt wise and lofty, as though by deciding to
die he had somehow been initiated into the mysteries of death—as
though it had, in some way, already taken place.

Then he walked to the window and hoisted himself onto the
ledge, making sure to maintain his expression as he did so, allowing only a brief grimace from the effort of the hoisting to intervene. Would the expression that was now on his face survive intact
after he died? Would it be imprinted on his corpse? Perhaps not,
he thought (for practical reasoning had not entirely abandoned
him), but he realized at once that such particulars were not the important thing, that what mattered was the spirit of it: that he meet
death with the proper expression was about something greater and
more significant than the look of his corpse.

Then again, it ought to look presentable.

And with this thought he got down from the ledge. From the
closet he took his fine suit and, frowning at the graveyard smudge,
wondered if it was suitable for his suicide. He put it on, looked at
himself in the mirror, then changed back into his regular work
clothes. But still something bothered him. He looked again at the
fine suit, and considered that in the case of a suicide, graveyard
smudges were actually not a disadvantage; the suit would be covered with blood anyway, and the smudge would only increase the
effect of gruesomeness.

He changed back into the fine suit, adjusted his hair in the
mirror, and stepped back onto the ledge.

But then, as soon as he was on it, he realized that his apartment, too, ought to be in suicide condition. He was bothered
by the fact that one of his dresser drawers was open by a few
inches, and the arm of a sweater was hanging out. He was
starting to get down, thinking that there was actually quite a
bit of tidying he could accomplish, when he stopped himself,

forcing himself to forgo any further preparations. These hesitations were unworthy of his suicide. He had decided to act and must act.

And, remaining on the ledge, to get himself back in the mood, he imagined once again the reaction to his death, the shock of the rubes in the office, the widened eyes of the coat-check woman, who might bring her hand delicately to her mouth . . . It would certainly give her something to talk about with Viola! . . . And to contemplate as she climbed those steep stairs up to the fourth floor . . .

But was he giving her all proper consideration?

He got back down from the ledge to consider this new problem more soberly. Just because he had made a resolution, that was no reason to be overly hasty.

He wondered if he should write a suicide note that could, by sly allusions, convey a message to the coat-check woman. But no, not to leave a note would be more mysterious—and he sighed with relief at not having to complete this extra task, which seemed very difficult. But if not a note, there should be *something* for her— some way for his obituary to call to her.

And all at once he hit on it. He sat at his desk, tore a pocket-size piece from one of the pages of his notebook, and wrote on it the numeral thirty-four. He looked at it with some satisfaction. He would place it in his pocket—but then he thought with dismay that it might be overlooked there. Perhaps the coroner—or would it be the responding officers?—would not be careful about combing for messages. He looked at his cuff, where the number could fit quite nicely, decided against it, then took off his shirt and wrote it in large numerals across the front before putting it back on.

Then he readjusted his expression back to that of the dignified suicide.

Before he got back up on the window ledge, he gave himself a kind of admonition, as though to say, "This is it . . . I'm not getting down from there again!"

But once he was back up, his thoughts again stopped him. Even the few minutes he had just taken to consider a message to the coat-check woman had made such a difference. What progress could he make with a few extra days of preparation—or even weeks? He could increase the mystery of his death tremendously! He could set up clues, false leads: a Borgesian labyrinth that in the end led nowhere, but tantalized all those who tried to understand it . . .

And, suddenly overcome by enchantment at this thought, he stepped down from the ledge once again.

He stood in front of the window, gradually submitting to the intoxication of the idea. What a suicide he could engineer for himself if he set his mind to it! And, a wide smile coming over his face, he walked slowly up to the window, and closed it.

He sat at his desk and opened his notebook, on fire with ideas for how his suicide could be hinted at and prepared for in the most mysterious manner imaginable. But his mind was too chaotic for him to begin to write; there were so many ideas dancing through it that he could not grasp at a single one, and, still smiling, he admonished himself to slow down, take a breath, this problem did not have to be solved in five minutes!

But he was too excited. Less by the specific ideas for how the suicide would be brought off—ideas for which, after all, there would be plenty of time—than by the way that his suicide, sparkling distantly in the future, would now bathe his life in an enchanting glow: every setback and inconvenience would now be not only bearable but actually a pleasure—each indignity would acquire the retrospective pathos of his coming demise.

For what could the uncouth remarks of his colleagues matter now? What power could joke-thinking glances have? He almost hoped the favor-askers would trouble him soon, so that he could smile the smile of his terrific, secret death when he acceded.

And all at once he relaxed deeply. There would be time enough to savor all these riches. He could wait months or perhaps even years; in fact, it was a kind of duty to wait, to be sure that he had explored every possible avenue before settling on the correct one. And anyway wouldn't his death itself be more effective if delayed, if it came randomly and seemingly without any antecedent, in many years?

Closing his notebook, he stood and took off his suit jacket and then his shirt, looking with a self-indulgent grin at the numeral with which he had emblazoned it. How silly he had been, in his haste!

And as he brushed his teeth and got ready for bed, he felt more and more firmly embedded within a calmness that was sturdier than any he had felt in quite some time. He was not without some exasperation at the thought of all the planning that was now ahead of him. No doubt a fabulous suicide would entail grueling efforts; elaborate logistical hurdles would have to be passed. But even this did not cause him undue distress. There was no obstacle that could outmatch the boundless faith he felt in himself.

And he went to bed smiling, imagining once again the knives falling on him with their pleasant stings—only now the pleasure of the stings was deeper and more satisfying, since the knives were to be the result of his own magnificent conception.

ACKNOWLEDGMENTS

For their indispensable assistance with this book, I am deeply grateful to Dan Milaschewski, Ryan Smernoff, Amanda Chiu Krohn, Makala Marsee, Todd Bottorff (and everyone else at Turner), Lisa Bankoff, Bruce Tracy, Adam Gopnik, Andy Borowitz, Simon Rich, Steve Hely, Ira Ungerleider, Adam Ehrlich Sachs, Shepard Boucher, John Bailey Owen, Matt Grzecki, Debra Stein, Jonathan Stein, Alex Stein, Ben Stein, Charlotte Thulin, and Lesley Thulin.

—N.H.S.

ABOUT THE AUTHOR

NATHANIEL STEIN HAS WRITTEN HUMOR AND nonfiction for the *New Yorker*, the *New York Times*, the *Los Angeles Review of Books*, and the *Daily Beast*, among other publications. He lives in Los Angeles where he works as a television writer. This is his first novel.